'*In the Cut* is surely one of the most underrated books of all time. Moore navigates the claustrophobic streets of a seedy New York and the dark, hidden avenues of female desire with equal grace, rewriting the thriller template with an elegance that proves totally devastating. She looks unflinchingly towards the darkness and finds beauty there as well as old, inescapable truths about what it means to be a reckless woman in a world of dangerous men'
Sophie Mackintosh, author of *The Water Cure*

'A remarkable novel that is erotic, intelligent, and daring'
Vanity Fair

'A master class in the writing of sex, the writing of death'
Irish Times

'Cruel and refined… gut-deep and risky … lurid, yet truthful, graceful, subtle and brutally intelligent … A story you will never forget'
Elle

'Extraordinary … A complicated thriller that taps fiction's deepest potential'
Time

'I was so mesmerised I stopped taking notes. I was in her power, and she could do whatever she liked'
Newsday

'An erotic thriller that described female sexuality in a way no man would know how to hazard'
Guardian

Susanna Moore is the author of the novels *The Life of Objects*, *The Big Girls*, *One Last Look*, *In the Cut*, *Sleeping Beauties*, *The Whiteness of Bones* and *My Old Sweetheart*, and two books of non-fiction, *Light Years: A Girlhood in Hawai'i* and *I Myself Have Seen It: The Myth of Hawai'i*. She lives in New York City.

IN THE CUT

SUSANNA MOORE

WEIDENFELD & NICOLSON

First published by Alfred A. Knopf, Inc. in 1995
This paperback edition first published in 2019 by Weidenfeld & Nicolson
an imprint of The Orion Publishing Group Ltd
Carmelite House, 50 Victoria Embankment
London EC4Y 0DZ

An Hachette UK Company

1 3 5 7 9 10 8 6 4 2

A CIP catalogue record for this book is
available from the British Library.

ISBN (trade paperback) 978 1 47461 360 6
ISBN (ebook) 978 1 4746 1362 0
ISBN (audio) 978 1 4746 1363 7

Printed and bound in Great Britain by
Clays Ltd, Elcograf S.p.A

www.orionbooks.co.uk

IN THE CUT

I don't usually go to a bar with one of my students. It is almost always a mistake.

But Cornelius was having trouble with irony.

The whole class was having trouble with irony. They do much better with realism. Realism, they think, is simply a matter of imitating Ernest Hemingway. Short flat sentences, an adjective before every noun. Ernest Hemingway himself, the idea of him that they have from the writing, makes them uncomfortable. They disapprove of him. They don't like him or the white hunter in "The Short Happy Life of Francis Macomber." The bravado, the resentment in the writing excites them, but they cannot allow themselves to feel it. Hemingway, they've decided, Hemingway, the person, isn't cool.

I considered giving them Naipaul to read, *A Bend in the River* or *Guerrillas*, but I decided that they would be so sensibly outraged by the beating, murdering and dismemberment of women that they might not be able to see the intelligence in the books. I wondered if they would like Graham Greene. *Brighton Rock* perhaps. But I had forgotten, I don't know how, the dream in which the murderer, straight razor in hand, says only two words: "Such tits."

Stream of consciousness, which some of them thought at first was stream of conscienceness, doesn't seem to give them much trouble. They think it's like writing down your dreams except without punctuation. Some of them admitted that before completing the Virginia Woolf assignment they'd smoked a little dope and it had helped. They make these confessions to me in a shyly flirtatious way, as if they were trying to seduce me. Which, of course, they are. Not sexually, but almost sexually. It would be sexual if they knew any better. And someday they will. Know better.

But irony terrifies them. To begin with, they don't understand it. It's not easy to explain irony. Either you get it or you don't. I am reduced to giving examples, like the baby who is saved from death in the emergency room only to be hit by a bus on the way home. That helps a little. Cornelius said that he preferred realism to irony because irony turned conceived wisdom on its head. Whether he meant to say conventional wisdom or received wisdom, I don't know. I was so distracted by an image of wisdom being turned on its head that I simply nodded and let him go on. Irony is like ranking someone or something, he said, but no one knows for sure you're doing it.

That's close enough, I said.

I am beginning to sound like one of the spinster ladies who used to take an interest in me in boarding school, except that they used to bemoan (a word they often used) the lack of manners, civility, and the incidence of haphazard breeding, rather than illiteracy. I hope that I don't turn into Miss Burgess in her good Donegal tweed suit, her snappish red terrier at heel, the dog's own tweed coat beginning to fray where it rubbed against his tartan leash. Summers in Maine with her companion Miss Gerrold in a cottage fragrant with mold. It doesn't seem that bad, now that I'm imagining it. Hydrangeas. Blueberries. Sketching on the rocks.

I admitted to my students that I am writing a book about regionalisms and dialects, including the eccentricities of pronunciation. I want them to know that I am not against dialect, or even misusage. I like it. I like that kids now think that Nike is a word of one syllable. Why wouldn't they? Nike isn't a goddess. It's a shoe. The winged shoe of victory. Despite my interest in idiomatic language, however, I do not want them to use phonetic spelling. I do not want to see motherfucker spelled mothafucka. Not yet. Get it right first, I said, then you can do whatever you like. It's like jazz. First learn to play the instrument.

Cornelius raised his hand last Tuesday and asked, I'm afraid, if I did not think my book on slang was a diss. A diss to whom? I asked. Stressing the whom.

Cornelius waited for me at the end of class. The others lingered around him, gathering their things slowly. He said, people like you think the brothers are guinea pigs. The way we talk and shit.

The others looked at me, no longer concealing their interest.

I walked out of the room.

He followed me.

The bars in my neighborhood fill me with dread. French tourists studying subway maps, and pink teenagers from Rockland County who look and talk like they're about to explode, perhaps with rage. I hope it is rage, since they have much to be angry about, even if they don't know it. The blank-faced thirteen-year-old girls with fake IDs and nose studs hoping to meet some sweet-talking Jamaicans; the black boys from the projects in those wide-legged shorts that hang below the knee, and Nautica windbreakers, the shorts making the elaborate running or hiking or telephone-lineman shoes that they wear look enormous and unwieldy, the boys jerking restlessly on the streets outside the bars with bottles of malt liquor in brown paper bags.

Just the thought of Bleecker Street makes me a little anxious. Stores full of baseball caps and silver-plated ankhs. Nowhere is there a sense of peace.

Cornelius and I sat at the bar in the Red Turtle. He took off his Walkman and ordered a rum and Coke. I said hello to Lothar, the bartender, and ordered a beer.

Cornelius gestured at the Walkman. "Smif and Wesson," I thought he said.

"Smith and Wesson? You're listening to guns?"

"Not Smith. Smif. It's regional. What you like."

He made me smile.

"And ironic," he said.

"I think it's you who's ironic."

I had once asked him if he would trash-talk for me, a form of humorous verbal intimidation. There are regional styles. In Chicago, for example, it is called signifying and it must be in rhyme. It hadn't been a success, Cornelius talking trash, or woofing as he calls it. He'd been inhibited. You can't just woof whenever you feel like it, he said.

He was having trouble with his term paper. That is why he wanted to see me. He didn't want to flunk another class, he said. He needed the credits.

I had asked my students to take a true story, a fact, a line from a newspaper or magazine, and turn it into fiction. An attempt to make them write about something other than themselves. It was called, rather grandly, The Re-created Event. I had encouraged them to look for a story in papers like the *National Enquirer*.

And Cornelius had. He wanted to know if he could turn his news clipping of the execution of John Wayne Gacy for the killing of thirty-three young men into an imagined conversation that he, Cornelius, had had with Gacy on the telephone. He wished to write about the sadness it had caused him to feel. Before his death, Gacy's voice could be heard on a 900-number by anyone interested enough to pay three dollars a minute to hear Gacy explain that he didn't kill those boys.

Cornelius told me he had spent close to forty-five dollars listening to the message.

I didn't know what to say.

"No," I said. "This is not supposed to be about you, Cornelius."

"You said in class once that every word a writer writes, even the conjunctions, even the punctuation you said, is a reflection of him or her."

"I don't think I said 'or her.' "

He smiled.

"I'm going to the bathroom," I said.

That was my second mistake.

I walked to the back of the bar. There was the smell of fried garlic and spilled beer. I did not see any bathrooms, or signs for bathrooms. I went down a flight of stairs to the basement. My eyes are not very good, so I put on my glasses. There were still no signs to help me along.

I opened a door into a room full of aluminum kegs of beer. I stopped at the next door. It was slightly ajar. I leaned against it, and the door opened slowly.

It was a small room. There was a metal desk. A coffee mug was on the desk, and a small lamp and a digital clock. The number on the clock changed with a loud, reluctant click. The lamp was made from a neon beer sign. In one corner was a jukebox, a plastic garbage bag thrown over it. There was an old sofa.

And there was a man sitting on the sofa.

His head rested against the wall, his face in darkness. I could see the rest of him clearly, illuminated in the small circle of pink light from the lamp. His suit jacket was on the back of the sofa. His tie was loose, one of those muddy-looking ties you can buy on the sidewalk in front of variety stores, displayed alongside the orderly arrangements of head-bands and blank cassettes. His hands lay on either side of him, indecorous, matter-of-fact, the pale palms turned upward in a gesture of supplication. There was a tattoo on the inside of his left wrist.

His legs were apart. Long. Slack. He wore black lace-up shoes and thin black socks, the kind of socks worn by a man who is vain about dress. His shoes needed a shine and that made me wonder about the vanity. There was an alluring symmetry to him, as if he were meditating, or balancing, or cajoling himself into what he knew would be uneasy sleep.

On the floor was a woman. Her hair was spread across his lap. She was kneeling, her hands on his thighs. She moved her head back and forth with a dipping motion as she took his cock into her mouth, then drew it out, then took him in again. I thought to myself, oh, I don't do it that way, with a hitch of the chin like a dog nuzzling his master's hand. The sound of her mouth was loud. She gave a little sigh and shifted her weight, quickening her movement. He lifted his head slowly and saw me standing in the doorway, my hands crossed on my chest as if I were about to be sacrificed.

He did not turn away. And he did not stop her. She made another little moan, just to let him know that she was getting tired, and he put his hands on top of her bobbing head, bunching up the red hair, gripping her, letting her know, letting me know, that he was about to come and he didn't want her to fuck it up by suddenly deciding to lick his balls.

I wanted to see his face. He could see mine.

He lifted her hair so that I could at least see his cock moving in and out of her mouth, her hand around him, sliding him up and down in time with her mouth. I could see that.

There was a stiffening in his thighs and she worked faster for a short quick time, and then there was a barely audible intake of breath as if he weren't going to give away any more than he had to, not even his breath, especially not his breath, and he held her head to him tightly. She began to slow down as he came, and I thought, this girl knows what she's doing.

I backed out of the room like a thief and he still did not turn away, his hands in her hair, holding her there so she could not see me, so it was just the two of us.

I did not go to the bathroom. I ran up the stairs, looking over my shoulder, suddenly afraid that someone had seen me standing in the doorway of the basement room.

Cornelius was not at the bar. He had ordered fried mozzarella sticks to take out. Said he had work to do. Something about a murder. Lothar winked at me. Haven't seen you in a while, he said.

When I paid the bill, I noticed that my hands were shaking.

It was a few days before I began to wonder why I kept forgetting to take my gray skirt to the tailor. I realized that I did not want to walk past the Red Turtle. I was keeping to my side of the park, what I think of as the Henry James side, even though those of us who live on the Square admit quietly amongst ourselves that he never lived on the Square. For a very short time, he lived around the corner on Washington Place, on the site of which there are now several quite handsome New York University dormitories.

I walked to the building on University Place where I teach twenty college freshmen what is optimistically called Creative Writing. (To my surprise, Cornelius was not in class. He seemed to be staying close to home, too.)

I walked to the market for half-and-half and cranberry juice. I walked to the post office on Thirteenth Street and Sixth Avenue where a radio is tuned to a rhythm-and-blues station and the line of silent, anxious customers snakes forward in step. I had to mail a book that I had borrowed, an *oeuvre érotique*, to my former husband, who is strict about things like borrowed books, as well as eroticism. He had written to remind me that I'd had the book for two weeks. The postal clerk, swaying in time to Sonny Boy Williamson, looked at the package and asked loudly, Santos Thorstin? *the* Santos Thorstin? Making me wonder if perhaps he had a better idea of who Santos Thorstin was than I had. My

Santos Thorstin is a fashion photographer who lives in Paris, but I had not realized that his reputation extended as far as the Thirteenth Street post office. Perhaps it was that series of photographs of murdered Bengali child prostitutes that had been turned into art postcards. I think often of something he once said to me: I'm sick of beauty. The clerk asked if it was true that I knew Santos Thorstin, and if I did, would I bring him in the next time he was in town?

So I kept to my side of the Square.

I live in two rooms on the third floor of a brownstone on Washington Square. As I have no doorman, and my parsimonious landlord pretends that there is no intercom system because it would ruin the design of the nineteenth-century front hall, it is impossible to control what my landlord calls the ingresses and egresses of the house. There are two doors to the house, one opening into the entrance hall, the second interior door leading to the stairs. I know that it is not a very safe system, just pushing the buzzer and allowing whoever has rung downstairs to come into the house. But I am lazy. Sometimes I am not properly dressed, or rushing to finish a paper, or expecting a friend, and it is easier to push the buzzer than to run downstairs.

When I was married to Santos Thorstin and lived in London, studying Middle English grammar, the hall porter tried to blackmail me. The mister would be so surprised, he said, by the gentleman who has come to call during his absence. So there is luxury in the knowledge that I may come and go, and my guests may come and go, without being noticed, although Pauline points out that I could be lying next to the six-slice toaster, a melted fork in my hand, every hair singed off my body, and it would be weeks, well, days before anyone found me. Fine with me, I told her.

In other words, had I known that it was Cornelius downstairs, wearing expensive camouflage, I might not have answered the bell. I cannot claim that I was expecting anyone, just that it was two-thirty in the afternoon—not an hour I usually associate with harm. I don't push the entrance buzzer at three in the morning.

He did not want to remove his Army jacket. He did not want to sit down, even though he thought my mother's steel garden chairs were cool. He did not want to stay. Only to give me money.

I was confused.

"From the bar," he said. "My half of the check."

He took six dollar bills from his pocket and put them on top of an open notebook on my desk.

"I tried to find you the other night," he said. "When you went to the bathroom. Where were you? I waited a long time."

"I couldn't find the bathroom," I said.

He stared at me. "Is that all?"

"All?"

"All I owe you."

I nodded, wanting him to go, turning away from him and putting my hand on the doorknob.

As I had chosen not to keep hours after class, I felt that it was unfair not to be accessible to my students in some way, especially since they were participants in a special city program for teenagers of what is called low achievement and high intelligence. One or the other of them often trails after me when I walk home. When we reach my stairs, I take out my keys and say, Until next week then. Do you think I should change my major? one of them will ask. To what? I ask. To writing; change it to writing books. Well, I answer slowly, if you're a writer, you'll know it. Who would choose to be a writer?

Perhaps foolishly, I had given them my address and telephone number. It would have been better, I see now, to have arranged to meet in one of the small rooms allowed to lecturers. There would have been boundaries. Restrictions. A clock on the wall. It would have been better than having Cornelius, dressed as a Green Beret, in my living room.

"I'm almost finished my paper," he said. "I want to show it to you. It would help and shit."

I hesitated.

"What you working on that's better?" he asked.

"I'm writing about language."

"Shit. You like that shit?"

"I do. I like, for example, that you add 'and shit' to the end of a sentence."

He was embarrassed and I realized that he thought I was making fun of him.

"You going to write that down? What I say?" he asked.

"Maybe. I'm interested in what you say. In what all of you say."

"Guinea pigs."

"No."

"You should be paying me."

"You think so?"

"Yeah," he said. "This is valuable shit, man." He sighed and put his hands in his pockets. "I'll do whatever you want. Chill if you want to chill, go to the store if you want to go to the store."

"I have work to do," I said. "That's what I want to do." I could hear horses, police horses going into the park.

"This is your scenario, man," he said.

He brushed against me as he went through the door, his black Ranger boots loud on the wood floor. I closed the door behind him, and locked it, and because the bolt makes a loud sound when it is turned, I knew that he would hear it sliding into its rusted grooves, and I was glad.

I went to the movies with my friend John Graham. We ate Thai noodles and shrimp at a restaurant on Thompson Street that is decorated to look like a grocery story in Shanghai. Pre-Mao. You can buy the props—bags of rice and Vietnamese fish sauce. He walked me home across the park, the Rasta drug dealers watching in noisy amusement.

I extended my hand, as always, and he took it and pulled me toward him to kiss me on the cheek, and said, good night, Frannie, and I said, the movie was good and that noodle place isn't so bad now that the models have moved on, and he agreed.

I closed the heavy street door behind me, pushing it with my shoulder to make sure that it was locked. I stooped to pick up the piles of Chinese menus that had been pushed under the door, and I saw a small white card sticking out of the corner of my mailbox.

It said Detective James A. Malloy. New York Police Department. There were two phone numbers in the top right corner.

Neither of which I thought I would call.

I used to keep a shopping bag full of the things that had been left on the stoop or pushed into my mailbox until the bag finally ripped at the sides. It had in it, among other things, a demo cassette of an elderly Welsh poet reciting eighteenth-century Cockney rhymes; a nude Barbie doll bound and gagged that my landlord brought upstairs to give to me—it had been on the Greek Revival doorstep all afternoon, he said warily, was it mine?—and a box of condoms, each one engraved or, more accurately, embossed with my name, the letter i dotted with a heart, a gift which I knew was meant for me, which I could not with absolute certainty say about the other gifts, and which I assumed had been left by someone I'd once dated.

So, needless to say, I threw Detective Malloy's card away.

By the time he knocked on my door two days later, I had forgotten about it. It was only when he handed me another card that I realized that the card in my box had, after all, been meant for me.

"Can I come in a minute?" he asked in a low pleasant voice. "It's better than talking in the hall." He looked over his shoulder as if someone were standing there, listening. He held his jacket by the back of the neck. His shirtsleeves were rolled to the elbow and there were wet half-moons under his arms. I wondered how he had gotten inside the house.

I was working on my monograph on Portuguese words in Rhode Island slang, but I felt that I couldn't use that as an excuse. I decided that if he noticed my notebooks, I'd say that I was writing in my diary. A safe girl-thing to be doing. Not that I had anything to hide from Detective Malloy. I just know from experience that trying to explain what it is that I write, what it is that interests me, makes me sound a little foolish, a little ineffective.

He held out the card until I took it, the card perhaps a way of letting me know that he really was a policeman, not a stockbroker in a paisley tie who spent his lunch hour bothering women. It occurred to me for a moment, being a resident of New York City, to ask to see his badge, but that would have embarrassed me.

I invited him inside.

"Nice place," he said, looking around quickly. "Been here long?"

"Not so long," I said. He was big. Tall. I could smell his cologne. It was strong and sweet, a little musk in it, a little drug-store, which usually gives me a headache. "Six months," I said. "I used to live on Seventy-first Street. Do you know that people once said they lived in a street, not on it? I lived *in* Seventy-first Street."

He smiled, and I realized something that he already knew. I was nervous.

He laid his jacket over the back of the sofa and sat in one of the steel garden chairs. The chair swings low to the ground when there is weight on it, and he looked startled when it dipped close to the floor for a moment. He reminded me of a ballplayer past his prime, the old muscles still twitching, just not so fast anymore. I couldn't imagine him chasing anyone down the street. But then detectives probably didn't do that.

"I'm doing a canvass in your neighborhood," he said.

He looked at the jade hairpins on the table. "There was a woman murdered on the sixteenth," he said. "That would be Tuesday the sixteenth. Last Tuesday sometime between midnight and two in the morning. Me and my partner are questioning people in the neighborhood. Her body—" He paused. "A part of her body, to be exact, was found across the street in the park here. I wanted to talk to you in case you saw or heard anything unusual. Saw anybody." He had a faint accent. He pronounced "saw" as if it had an r at the end of it. He lengthened his vowels, stretching the second vowel so that "exact" sounded like exaaact.

"There are hundreds of people in the street at night," I said. "All night long."

He nodded. "We came by the other day," he said, "me and my partner, but you must of been out."

He looked at the jade hairpins again, each a different shape. They had belonged to a Chinese maid in my grand-mother's house in San Francisco, whom I think of tenderly as the only person, as far as I know, that my mother ever loved. When I was a child, I'd thought the pins must have belonged to a queen. Later, when I saw the kind of hairpins used by rich Chinese women, the pins covered with knobs of coral that looked like raw meat, carved with inscriptions beseeching male children and long life, they were not as beautiful as the pale jade sticks.

"What are they?" he asked, picking them up and holding them in his outstretched hand.

"Guess. No one has ever guessed correctly."

"No one?"

He was interested in this game, I could tell.

"Utensils," he said. "Utensils of some kind."

"In a way," I said. I wondered if he had a gun.

"They're old," he said. "Jade. Are they for a female?"

"No questions allowed," I said.

He was suddenly bored. "Tell me," he said.

I shook my head, and I realized that he'd been trying to work up the interest to flirt with me. His eyes were the kind of blue that would change with the light, or the color of his shirt. They were, at the moment, opaque.

"No," I said.

He sighed in dismissal and stood up, the chair swaying beneath him. "My ex-wife collects dolls," he said. He put the hairpins back on the table, lining them up absentmindedly, and I suddenly wondered if he was neat. I imagined that he, too, had a collection of dolls. Lined up neatly.

"Did you see or hear anything, by the way?" he asked. "The night of the sixteenth, morning of the seventeenth? You never answered me."

He picked up his jacket and took a pen and a small stenographer's pad from the inside pocket. He flipped the pad open with one hand. He saw me looking at the pen. It was a maroon Mont Blanc ballpoint. He held it out to me.

"Fake," he said. "It's a cop thing." He winked.

"No, I didn't see or hear anything unusual," I said. "I sleep with the windows open."

"Do you?" he asked, looking up from the pad. "All the way open?"

"Who was killed?" I asked. "Not my landlord, I know." I was surprised by my flippancy. I was still nervous. But now I knew why.

"An actress. Twenty-six years old. She worked part-time in a after-hours gambling club. She was last seen in a bar around the corner. A cop bar, as a matter of fact."

"A cop bar?"

"Yeah," he said. "It's the Sixth Precinct bar. A lot of detectives go there."

"I'm sorry," I said. "Sorry that she was killed."

He nodded.

"How was she killed?"

"Her throat was cut." He paused. "And then she was disarticulated."

What a good word, I thought. Disarticulated.

He slid the notebook back into his pocket and took two cuff links from another pocket and turned down the sleeves of his shirt, and I remembered that it was masculine gestures that aroused me.

He looked at me as he pushed one of the cuff links through the hole. "You remind me of someone," he said.

I was disappointed in him. "I'm not surprised. I have that kind of face."

That kind of ass, I thought.

"You'll let me know if you remember anything? My office number is on the card. Call anytime."

He walked to the door. I opened it for him.

His trousers were a little tight. Thin black socks. Black shoes, lace-up. Needed a shine. A small tattoo inside his wrist. The three of spades. But no redhead between his legs.

I dreamed about him that night.

It was near morning, really. There was faint light behind the wooden shutters. It was that time when I am finally able to sleep the sweetest, the deepest. My skin feels smooth against the sheets and I wonder why it takes until dawn to feel so smooth. It is the same leg, the same sheet, as it was eight hours earlier.

I pushed aside my pillows and turned onto my stomach. My feet hung off the end of the bed, my toes hooked over the edge. The way I do. And through my cotton nightgown, I put two fingers of my right hand on my clitoris and thought of him. Standing in a room, coming toward me, watching me undress. (It must always be through a nightgown or a pair of underpants. I've wondered if this is because of the greater friction. Surely that must be part of it, but there is something more, perhaps the thrill that first came to me as a small girl, pressing my fingers against myself, the cloth interceding between my fingers and my vagina, interceding between shame and pleasure. Perhaps I was afraid that I would die were there not a piece of cloth, something intervening, to prevent me from falling irrevocably into a trance of self-delighting.)

One Sunday morning in boarding school I found my roommate lying on her back on the tile floor of the shower stall. Her legs, covered with black and blue bruises from hockey, were splayed on either side of the spigots, the water cascading between her slack muscular thighs. I couldn't imagine what she was doing. I thought that she had slipped on the wet tiles. She remains to this day the only woman I've ever known who spoke freely of her own masturbation. She urged me to try it. I didn't have the courage to tell her that I had found my own way. Women will talk about anything—sexual jealousy, dishonor, the lovely advantages of eating pussy or sucking cock, the disadvantages of eating pussy or sucking cock—but they will not tell you about fucking themselves.

So there was Detective Malloy, watching me take off my clothes.

My clitoris swelled under my fingers. My breath grew short. My legs stiffened. Inside, I rose and rose, sometimes stopping short, but not without pleasure even in the prolongment. It is not the same as when a man's fingers are there and I do not know if he will have the skill or the patience or the interest to see it through, the not-knowing causing my body to overreach, to strain too hard. I am confident when it is my hand. Sometimes I am greedy, and I get a terrible cramp in my calf and I have to leap up and limp around the room until it goes away.

Malloy was happy to wait.

This morning when I left the house, walking to the subway at Astor Place, I noticed two men sitting in a dull gray car. I noticed it because the color of the car was without shine, as if it had been sanded, and I noticed it because there is no street parking during the day on Washington Square.

Before I had time to think about this, not even realizing yet that it warranted thinking about, there was the rough grating sound of the bottom of a car door scraping against cement, and a voice said, "Oh, Miss."

He stood with one black shoe on the curb, his arm resting on the open door. Another man sat in the driver's seat.

"Hi, how you doing? Could we talk to you a minute?"

He leaned forward and opened the door to the back seat.

"I'm supposed to get in?" I asked.

"It wouldn't hurt," he said in a low voice. "Unless you want to talk in the street. I never think it's a good idea to put your business in the street, you know what I'm saying? But it's up to you." His hand fell away from the door handle, as if he thought less of me for my hesitation.

My business in the street? I thought. What is he talking about?

I got into the car.

"My eyes aren't very good," I said as he closed my door with two hands and eased himself back into the front seat. "Someday I'm going to get into the wrong car."

"That wouldn't be smart," he said, watching a white boy buy dope from one of the Jamaicans. "This is my partner, Detective Rodriguez," he said.

Detective Rodriguez turned to look at me. "Hi, how you doing?" Another big handsome man. Black hair, black eyes. Big head. White shirt. Silver tie. A black jacket on a hook in the back next to me. This is someone who has spent some time at Club Broadway, I thought, and not at the six o'clock beginners' merengue class.

"Hello, Detective Rodriguez. How do you do?"

The radio was on, a regular radio, not a police radio, and that interested me. Marvin Gaye, turned low, not a police dispatcher. I had read that detectives sometimes ate raw garlic before questioning a witness, so this didn't seem too bad. I sat forward and crossed my arms on the back of the front seat, between the two of them. Malloy looked at me for a moment when I suddenly appeared at his shoulder, then turned away to roll down his window.

"We wanted to ask you some questions," said Rodriguez.

"One of your neighbors heard screams in MacDougal Alley the night in question." He leaned forward to wipe the inside of the windshield.

"The night in question," I said. "There are screams almost every night in MacDougal Alley."

Detective Rodriguez looked at me in the rearview mirror. "You a teacher?"

I nodded.

"You run those prints?" Malloy suddenly asked him.

"What's an isthmus?" Rodriguez said, still watching me in the mirror.

"Isthmus be my lucky day. You ran the prints. And?"

"And nothing."

"Jesus," Malloy said under his breath.

"We just wanted to double-check with you," Rodriguez said, turning so that I could see his face and he could see mine. "In case there was something you forgot. You know, sometimes things come back."

I did stop to think, just to be polite, lowering my eyes to appear to concentrate better, and I noticed that Detective Rodriguez wore a holster at his waist. It was brown leather, and the island of Puerto Rico was painted on it in green and red. That in itself was enough to get my attention, as well as my admiration, but what really interested me was that in the holster was a yellow plastic water pistol.

"To tell you the truth," Rodriguez said, "the reason Detective Malloy and I thought you might be able to help is that a Mr."—he looked down at a piece of paper lying on the seat between them—"Lothar Wilker, an employee in a bar called the Red—"

"—Turtle," said Malloy.

"—Turtle, says you were there the evening of the sixteenth. The night in question."

Malloy turned to look at me.

"Yes," I said. "I was there with one of my students. I was there for a very short time, and came home."

"What's his name?" Malloy asked.

"Whose name? My student?"

"Yeah, your student."

"Cornelius Webb."

"Did you leave the bar alone?" Rodriguez asked. "I mean, did you go home alone?"

I hesitated. I wanted to tell him that it was none of his business. "Yes."

"Did you happen to notice a young female," Malloy asked, "mid-twenties, not too tall? Red hair. Good-looking." He turned to Rodriguez. "Wouldn't you say?"

"What?"

"She was good-looking."

"Not bad," Rodriguez said. "Were you in the front room the whole time?" He asked me. He looked out the window, picking his teeth with a match.

"Front room?"

"The bar area."

"Yes."

He looked at me in the mirror. "You sure?"

"I tried to go to the bathroom," I said, "but I couldn't find it."

"The bathroom?" asked Malloy.

"I thought you said you stayed in the bar," Rodriguez said. "I forget," he said to Malloy. "Did she say that?" He turned back to me. "The deceased was also seen in the Red Turtle that night. That's why we're checking again with you. Seeing as how you was there. You wouldn't object to looking at some pictures, would you? Maybe a lineup down the way?"

"She don't see too good," Malloy said to him.

I wondered how Malloy knew that I didn't see too well, and then I remembered that I had said so as I got into the car.

Rodriguez turned to Malloy with a smile and said, "A day without death is a day without sunshine." He took a color photograph from his pocket and held it so that I could see it. "She look familiar?"

I'd seen her before. "No," I said. "I'm sorry."

"Me, too," Malloy said.

Rodriguez put away the photograph, no longer interested.

Malloy hit the side of the door with one hand and the door popped open. He leaned over stiffly and opened my door.

He walked after me a few steps, his hands in his pockets. It caused his trousers to rise around his ankles.

"I wondered if you wanted to go out for a beer or something," he said quietly. "There's a bar on Sheridan Square where my cousin's the bartender. You might of been there already. He says a lot of writers go there."

"Now?" I was surprised. I glanced back at the car. The runner-up in the Mr. Puerto Rico contest was cleaning his nails with a small knife.

Malloy laughed. "Not now." He had mistaken my confusion for eagerness.

"How do you know I'm a writer?" I asked.

"I can tell," he said. "You're making shit up in your head all the time."

We struggled in class this afternoon with the polemical style. I thought that they wouldn't like it, but to my surprise they seem to prefer it to other styles of writing. They are, of course, full of their own polemic. They are scared out of their wits, but they disguise it with a noisy, melodramatic pessimism. I gave them Orwell, Tolstoy and Bret Easton Ellis to read.

Cornelius waited for me on the street after class.

"Where you going?" he asked.

"I'm going to Astor Place," I said. "To the subway."

He walked beside me, walking the walk. "How's that dictionary thing you making?"

"Why weren't you in class last week?"

"My head, man. I get spells. Head-spells."

I raised my eyebrows.

He slapped his hand down hard on a parking meter. "You think I'm lying? You don't believe me?"

"No," I said.

"Man," he said, shaking his head. "I want to help you and you all is telling me I'm a liar."

"How could you help me?"

"Tell you shit. Secret words and all."

I hesitated, not sure if it was a good idea to have Cornelius tell me shit.

"You wouldn't have to pay nothing," he said.

We reached the stairs to the subway. "Maybe," I said. "We'll see. Do your term paper first."

"My murder-scape."

"Your murder-scape."

I went down the stairs, and when I looked back, he was standing there, watching me.

Two women sitting next to me on the subway were talking about a man. One of the women said, he just want to conversate and I just want to blowse through my magazine. I could kill that man.

A dangerous combination for me. Language and passion.

I have often noticed that words that are incorrectly rendered have an onomatopoetic logic, as well as a kind of poetry, that is more appealing, sometimes even more accurate, than correct usage. The wrong words are sometimes so close to a truer meaning that they are like puns. Many of the words have to do with the body, or disease. For example, Old Timer's Disease, rather than Alzheimer's. Abominal for stomach. Athletic fit for epileptic fit. Chicken pops. Very close veins. The prostrate gland.

And there are other words, too. Daily-by-daily. Chomping at the bit. Autumn furlage. Unchartered waters. And what could be more alluring than breastesses?

The women left the train. I looked up and saw that the Poetry in Motion placard had been changed. The new poem was in Spanish with an English translation. It was by García Lorca, full of words like *remanso*, which means still waters, and *fronda de luceros*, or frond of stars. But the word that thrilled me was *espesura*. I whispered it many times, breaking it into syllables, trying it this way and that, rushing it, slowing it down, until I noticed a boy staring at me in boredom.

Espesura, or thicket. Also a beautiful word, thicket. As in *bajo espesura de besos*. Under a thicket of kisses.

I was going to have supper with Pauline, who lives farther downtown than I do. Her building has the added advantage of a topless club on the ground floor. Although the cinderblock walls of the club are soundproofed and painted with what feels like twenty coats of tar, Pauline is kept awake at night by the music. Barbra Streisand. Barry Manilow. Gloria Gaynor. Sometimes she can't help herself and dances to the music in the dark.

When I first knew her, fifteen years ago in London, she made a living by finding and selling paintings. Sometimes a piece of furniture. Each year it grew a little more difficult because, as she put it, there was nothing left in the world to which some value had not been attached. Even shit, she said. She'd found it hard to compete with the new buyers. I admired her discernment, and her stubborn refusal to stoop to what she considered art, which for her was a category that included most things made before 1939. She was an aesthetic snob.

Pauline has seven elaborate locks on her door. It takes her several minutes to open them. She handed me a glass of champagne as I came in, a reward for having to wait so long on the landing, listening to "Windmills of My Mind." A favorite on the jukebox downstairs. After all, it was Happy Hour at the Pussy Cat. Or Unhappy Hour, as Pauline says. The early evening jukebox selections tended to the maudlin, which always surprises me, sentimentality being an emotion that for me usually attends later in the night.

"Sit down," she said, lifting a pile of magazines from the chenille sofa. Pauline reads every magazine in the world.

She was wearing red and white gingham capri pants and a mohair brassiere. She has a soft, ample mouth which she claims is one of the most misleading things about her in a swamp of misleading things. Men tend to think, and to tell her, that her mouth holds a promise of proficiency, only they don't put it quite that nicely. In fact, as she is quick to point out, she has in her own observations ascertained that the size, the construct, the suggestiveness of just about anything has nothing, regrettably, to do with its efficacy. Her mouth, she says apologetically, is not one of her areas of particular expertise. No one, however, seems to take her word for it, and her mouth, as a consequence, tends, overall, to cause her more trouble than it is worth.

She sees the diminished side of most things—she speaks of herself often (and in mixed company, as Miss Burgess would say) as a slut. She refers resignedly to her inability to find true love as if it were a congenital weakness or fair punishment for some feminist principle that she mistakenly espoused in late adolescence and cannot now abandon honorably.

"You know," she said modestly, sounding as if we were finishing a conversation rather than starting one, "my accent took me a long way in America, but I didn't last ten minutes in London. They knew exactly who and what I was. A little Irish Protestant scrubber. But here. Well. You could even say my accent took me rather too far. People think I'm much more than I am."

"At least you had an accent. I wish I'd had something to take me a long way. I grew up in embassy kitchens. I was completely unprepared for New York. No one had warned me that New York is like a big dinner party. You have to be very careful about what you say and do because you never know whose feet are touching under the table. I got into a lot of trouble in the beginning."

"Yes," she said. "I've always thought that you tell the truth far more than is necessary." She smiled with a kind of abashed formality, embarrassed by revelation. There was a thwarting of words on her tongue, in her mouth.

Abashed is a good word.

"On the street tonight," I said, "I heard a man shout 'You the one.' "

"Were you?"

"No. Sorry to say. I'm afraid the one was a beautiful boy."

"I have something for you," she said. "A present. It's brought me bad luck, so it's time to pass it on to you."

She left the room, and when she returned she held a brocade bag in her hand. She took my hand and lifted the bag and shook it, and into my hand fell a heavy gold bracelet. There were five gold charms on the bracelet.

"It's Cartier," she said, sitting down. She folded the bag neatly and slipped it beneath the vinyl cushions of her chair.

I took off my glasses to look at the bracelet. There was a tiny baby carriage. A cocktail shaker. A telegram.

"It belonged to my aunt. The only interesting person in my family."

There was a gold toilet, and a tiny utensil that looked like it might be a poultry bulb-baster.

"What is this?" I asked, holding the bulb-baster out to her. It is a hard thing to say, bulb-baster. Ball-buster, on the other hand, is easy to say. The handle of the toilet was set with a sapphire.

"It was given to my aunt," she said, "by a man. I don't know who he was. She would never tell me."

She was bemused and calm. Becalmed. She gave me a slightly sinister smile. "Open the cocktail shaker."

I did. Inside was a little gold baby. I tipped it into my palm.

I stared at her, not understanding. But beginning to understand. Shocked. "A lover gave her this?"

She nodded, pleased at my distress.

"Did he think that she would wear it?" I asked.

"She *did* wear it. I remember it when she played cards. I thought the baby and the carriage were adorable. Maybe that's why she left it to me."

I sat back in my chair. I did not know what to say. When I could speak, I said something that surprised even me: "Most things, I've come to believe, are not intended."

She gave me a look as if she were disappointed in me. "Can you imagine him going into Cartier and ordering it? It is not as if they have charms for the termination of pregnancy in the display case. Well, perhaps now they do, but they didn't have them in 1956. The charms would have been made especially for him. Can you imagine! Who was this guy? He sounds like someone I might have gone out with."

I stared at her, trying to decide if her smile could be called ghastly (I thought it could), or if she really was amused by her story.

"I'll wear it," I said in some impetuous, unwished-for pledge of female honor, a gesture of defiance on behalf of her aunt, the only interesting person in her family.

"I knew you would," she said. "We're having nasturtiums and cheese for dinner. You don't mind, do you?"

"Of course not," I said.

I came through the door into one of those warm strong breezes blowing from the river. The neon sign of the winking cat biting the tip of its tail turned the chrome of the cars to pink. The heavy brass-studded door of the Pussy Cat opened for a moment as two men wearing baseball caps went inside, and I could hear Whitney Houston singing one of her high school graduation songs.

Cornelius was across the street, having a conversation with a doorman.

They stopped talking the moment they saw me, as if they were speaking some language I couldn't even begin to understand. And they probably were.

The doorman made a gesture of tipping his hat to me. I thought of pointing it out to Cornelius as an example of irony, but I didn't.

I turned away from them, not speaking, walking, liking the way that the hot wind felt on my face, feeling the weight of my new bracelet on my wrist. I heard Cornelius cross the street. He caught up with me.

"Just passing by?" I asked, not looking back.

"We were talking."

"What about?"

"Chicks."

I nodded, turning the corner.

"You think it's right," he said, "that chicks act the way they do, you know, like captives, 'cause they be scared of male violence?"

I turned to look at him. "That's what you were talking about just now?"

He laughed. "Fuck that shit. We were talking about *chicks*." He walked alongside me. "Where you going?" He let his backpack slide from his shoulder to his elbow and put his Walkman inside, pretending to be busy, pretending that it was perfectly all right that I should find him waiting for me at eleven o'clock at night at the corner of White and Chapel streets. He fastened the buckle of his backpack.

"Where you going?" he asked again.

"What are you doing here, Cornelius?"

"I waited for you."

"You followed me, you mean."

He turned his cap on his head. Getting the right pose. Profiling, as he would say.

"I got on the same train as you, in the next car. I was going to my grandma's in Brooklyn but when the car stopped at Canal I saw you get out, and I got out, too." He paused. "There ain't nothing wrong with that," he said.

"Well," I said slowly, "I think that there is. Something wrong with that."

"I got words for you and shit."

I did not necessarily disbelieve him, but I still did not think it a good idea that he had followed me. And waited for me. Three hours. To give me words.

"You might not want them 'cause they be words for— you know," he said slyly.

"What?" I asked.

"You know."

"I don't know. What are you talking about?"

"Words for that. What you calls sex."

I wanted to ask him what he called it. We were at the corner of Broadway and Franklin. "Look, Cornelius," I said. "I think you should go on to your grandmother or wherever it is that you go. I don't want to do the dictionary with you anymore."

"I don't want to go home," he said, as if he were telling the truth at last. I wondered in sudden detachment if I would at last find out what it was that he wanted from me.

"Why not?" I asked.

"The man was there. He come to scarify my grandmother about some dead bitch. There's another murder, he said. He going to a murder."

"He going to a murder?" I repeated.

"He got no right to ask me no questions and shit," he said petulantly.

"It's about that murder. A girl who was in the bar was murdered. That's what he wants to talk to you about."

"What bar? I don't go to no bars."

"We went there after class," I said patiently, wondering why I was patient with him.

"What's up with that, man?"

"The bartender knows me," I said. "He gave the police my name."

"But how he know me? What the fuck I need that shit for?"

"I don't know, Cornelius. I don't care. I told the detective I was there with one of my students."

We reached the stairs to the subway.

"I'm going uptown with you," he said. "You can't be on the Six this time of night."

He followed me down the stairs. A train was pulling in

and I quickly put in my token and he jumped the stile and we were on the train in a rush of triumph that was unsuitable the moment the doors bounced shut behind us. There were six other people in the car, three of them tired women who looked as if they were headed home after cleaning the empty office buildings on Wall Street. I noticed that the Poetry in Motion poem was new. An excerpt from *The Passionate Man's Pilgrimage*. Walter Ralegh. "Give me my Scallop shell of quiet."

Cornelius smiled at me. I suddenly wondered if he thought that I was powerless, and then I realized that I *was* powerless. Of course, I could always jump off the train at the next stop and find a transit cop to complain that a student of mine was insisting on accompanying me home at night for my own safety. That would be an interesting exercise.

We didn't speak, standing because I thought that to sit would imply ease and even intimacy, swaying with the train, knees bent slightly in the way of subway travelers. The train stopped at Astor Place and we got off.

"Why they got a design of beavers on the wall here?" he asked. He was behind me. "I know you know," he said.

I did know.

"But you ain't saying," he said. " 'Cause you be vexed at me."

A word his West Indian grandmother might use. Vex. Like cutlass. Probably brought to the Caribbean by Walter Ralegh, who was now in the subway.

"I'm safe now, Cornelius," I said over my shoulder, going quickly up the stairs.

I walked down Eighth Street toward Fifth Avenue. I

wanted to stop at the deli to buy milk for the morning, but I kept walking.

"I got you this far," I heard him say.

As I reached the end of the block, I noticed a car parked in front of my building. It was a gray car, rusted at the fenders. A man was leaning against it.

I suddenly realized that the sound of Cornelius's step had ceased. I turned around. He was gone.

I pretended that I did not see him. I went up the stairs.

He called my name.

I turned around.

He was below me, on the sidewalk, bouncing keys in his open hand.

"I was hoping you were in," he said.

"I'm not in."

"You're not?"

He made me smile.

"I just wanted to check a few more things with you," he said.

"A few things?"

"That's right. A few things."

"Do you want to come in?" I asked, surprised at myself.

"No," he said.

I realized that I wanted him to come inside. Which surprised me even more. A decision, any decision, tends to bring flirtation to an end. Marriage, a quintessential decision, being a good example.

"It won't take a minute," he said. He turned and opened the car door near the curb.

I came slowly down the stairs, knowing that he was watching me, the deliberation of movement, the slow sway of hip, one hand in my pocket, the other holding the hair back from my face. I took off my glasses.

I got into the car.

He said, "Still getting into cars with strange men."

The radio was turned to an oldies station. He walked around the car and got inside, moving as if his body were sore. "I been in the fucking tunnel all day," he said.

"A fucking tunnel?" Sometimes I hear language in a way that causes me to appear to be more literal than I am.

He looked at me. "We got a call. There's a dead body in the tunnel that runs along the West Side Highway. Where I used to watch the circus trains when I was a kid. Now it's a place for homeless people. Hungarian Gypsies mostly. I didn't even know there was Gypsies left, did you?"

I shook my head.

"We find a mummified body. He's a mummy *and* he's got numerous stab wounds all over him."

I said nothing, fearful that he would stop. He seemed to be talking to himself. A meditation, an ordering of thought.

"First off," he said with what looked like a smile, "we think that the guys from the Two-Oh found the body, then dragged it into the next precinct. We do it all the time. We find a floater and we kick and slap the water so it'll float to another precinct so we don't have to deal with it. So I went to find my old friend, Vladimir Kostov. It's taken me years to enter his little domain. He collects water as it drips down from Riverside Park. He says the rocks filter it. He pisses round his things 'cause he says rats won't cross the line. I almost killed him the first time I saw him. He charged me with a knife. He hates everyone in the world, but he took a liking to me. And he told us about the body. It turns out the mummy's name is Farrington. We had to cut his fingers off."

"I'm sorry," I said.

"Usually the M.E. does it. Cuts off the fingers and soaks them to get prints. When you get mummified, you lose all the fluid in your body and the skin on the fingers collapses, you know what I'm saying? You don't get good prints. It happens with fire victims, too. You have to skin the finger, then turn it inside out and put your own finger inside the skin and roll it back down so's you can read the print backward. Now this Farrington was a bad guy. He was locked up once for homicide. He also turned out to be a pimp for a male pross, a transvestite named Michael Tilly or Miss Theresa, depending on which one he was that day." He sighed and ran his fingers through his hair. "I found Miss Theresa this afternoon in a SRO on East 126th Street, dying of AIDS. He's got explosive diarrhea and he's throwing up at the same time he's going from Michael Tilly to Miss Theresa and to a third pross named Miss Honey. He's fucked-up. But I start talking to him and slowly, eventually, I begin to put it together. Miss Honey killed Farrington because she was afraid of him. He was taking her money, slapping her around. Making her blow all sorts of people, the prick."

I was confused.

"Anyways," he said, "I left him there to try to get Social Services to put him in a hospital. When I went back, he was dead. *She* was dead. *They* were dead."

"Cornelius says there's been another murder near here," I said.

"Who?"

"Cornelius Webb. My student."

"Now why would he tell you that?"

"I don't know," I said, wondering myself.

"What did he tell you?" There was a change in his voice. He was alert. No longer dreamy, no longer anecdotal.

"That another woman was killed."

"When did he tell you this?"

"He said that you told his grandmother. He said that you said that you were going to another murder."

He looked at me. "Another funeral, maybe," he said. "Not another murder. There's been two women murdered in Manhattan South in the last seventeen days. What does that tell you?"

I didn't think that I should answer flippantly. About men and women, that is. I said nothing.

"I'll tell you what it tells you. One killer isn't doing all of them."

He was both veiled and exact. Selective, but not averse to giving a suggestive illustration. "Multiple killers have a thing, a way to kill effectively that they use over and over again. It's like anything. We all do it. We use what works, and usually it's the easy way. A killer learns on the job. He gets better at it. But he'll do it the same each time. These two homicides were different. Different styles."

I looked out the window at two young girls walking slowly along the edge of the park, looking for trouble.

"Why did you become a policeman?"

He looked at me, surprised. "I don't know. I just did. Listen, when did he say I was going to another murder?"

I didn't know if he was asking when Cornelius had told

me or when he was supposed to be going to another murder. "About ten minutes ago," I said.

He nodded. "I *believe*," he said, "I *believe* what I said to Mrs. Webb is I was going to another funeral."

I looked at him.

"A funeral," he said. "Not quite the same thing, you know what I'm saying?"

I could smell his cologne or his aftershave, whatever it was that he was wearing, and I suddenly remembered that my father used to say, Gentlemen don't wear scent. This wasn't scent. The air-conditioning was on, and it was cold inside the car. It made the smell stronger. I rolled down the window, and he leaned forward and turned off the air conditioner.

He reached beneath his suit jacket as if he had an itch and pulled out a small black beeper and tried to make out the number on it, leaning forward to catch the light from the streetlamp. He sighed, and clicked off the beeper, hooking it with difficulty back onto his waistband. "It wasn't that kid you were walking with just now, was it?" he asked. "That black kid. Cornelius."

"You've been following me, too," I said.

"Following you?" He laughed.

He turned up the radio. "It's in His Kiss." Betty Everett. I looked at his hands. He wore a big gold ring on the third finger of his left hand, like a college ring. On the little finger of his right hand was a small gold ring, two hands holding a heart. Mick shit. I wondered if he had a shamrock on his ass.

"Where you from?" he asked suddenly. Before I could answer, he said, "I'm from Washington Heights." He stopped to listen to the music. "You know, there was nothing better than, when you were a kid, you know, making out and shit."

I was silent, refusing to give him the advantage he'd just taken.

"You from the city?" he asked.

"The Philippines," I said.

He looked at me in interest. "Get the fuck out of here!"

"Yes," I said. "It's a terrible country."

"Get the fuck out of here!"

"My father was in the State Department."

"No shit."

"Whose funeral are you going to?"

He laughed again. "I'm not going to no funeral. Not tonight anyways. I've been to a lot of funerals, but not too many at night. I was at an autopsy today, does that count?"

"Maybe."

"That girl who was murdered last week." His voice became low and intimate. "You know, if someone is killed by manual strangulation or blunt force trauma to the stomach, it might not be visible the first time you look at it. I can examine the body at the scene and not know for sure. I can say this looks like a homicide, this smells like a homicide, this *is* a homicide, but that don't mean I know *why* it's a homicide. Nobody can enter a crime scene without changing it in some way—adding to or taking away. Usually adding to it. You know what I'm saying? But bodies talk to me. A dead body can tell me lots of things. All I need to know, sometimes."

He turned down the radio.

"Listen," he said. "I've been going back over that girl's homicide. The redhead. That's why I came by. There's something missing. A piece. Something I know that I don't know yet."

"Disarticulation," I said.

"How do you know that?" he asked, looking at me curiously.

"You told me. I looked it up."

"You confuse me," he said.

"Confuse you?"

"I thought I was going to buy you a beer."

He stood at the bar and pulled out a stool. I sat down and he asked what I wanted and I said a beer, hoping he wouldn't ask what kind of beer, quickly adding, whatever you're having. He ordered two Guinnesses and put a twenty-dollar bill on top of the bar. It was not something a woman would do, lay money on a bar like that. I am very interested in the ways that men are different from women.

"Do you still live in Washington Heights?" I asked.

"I never left Washington Heights. Not really. I tried, Jesus, Mary and Joseph, I tried, but I didn't get too far. I have to cross the George Washington Bridge two times a day when I come in to work. I know I've been a New York City detective too long when I can feel my stomach start to turn the minute I get off the bridge in Manhattan. I actually get sick to my stomach now. My old partner used to say, Malloy, you got to get out when it's no fun no more. You'll know when it's over the day it's no fun anymore. You know what I'm saying?"

"I do," I said.

He looked around the bar. He had chosen the far end, and he stood facing the front door. He was wearing, I noticed, what looked like a tie from Hermès, one of those ties that rich boys wear with a design of animals on it. Giraffes or anteaters. He saw me looking at it.

"A gift," he said. "A gift from a East Side DOA. You like it?" He lifted the end to look at it. He liked it.

"A gift?" I didn't understand.

"Look," he said with a smile, "I been two steps away from prison my whole life."

"You still haven't told me where you live."

"Rockland County. You know where that is? Upstate New York. Other side of the Hudson." His arm brushed against my knee and he said, "Pardon me."

He reached for the big glass of Guinness and I noticed again the beauty of his hands, the wrists, the clean plain nails. The tattoo.

He saw me looking at his hands.

"I got faggot hands," he said.

I wondered if he felt the same way about his eyes. Faggot eyes. I had a feeling that he liked his eyes.

"What about the tattoo?"

"I'm in a club. A secret club."

"Are there a lot of members?"

"Just a couple."

I nodded. Pretty much what I'd thought.

"I live with my ex-wife. To answer one of your many questions." He took a drink and wiped a line of pale foam from his lip.

For some reason, I wasn't surprised.

"I went back five years ago. To tell the God's honest truth,

I was exhausted. When I got divorced, I lived with my mother in Washington Heights, surrounded by Dominicans. It was a little embarrassing being divorced and living with your mother, you know what I'm saying? not knowing how to say it at the end of an evening, you know, we got to go to your place 'cause my mother might be up saying the rosary, I promise I'll be gone by morning."

"Not a bad idea."

He looked surprised.

"Leaving before morning," I said.

"A woman don't want you to spend the night, either, right? Women don't want to wake up with some big lug in the morning. I have to be at work at four in the afternoon some days. She don't want you around all fucking day. Many women that I know take you home, you make love, it's all over, you get up, you can see the relief on their faces: Not only does he fuck me well, he leaves. You don't want to wake up in the morning and see her, either. Everybody's happy."

He gave me a big smile and picked up his glass of beer. I picked up my glass, too, and the charm bracelet made a sound on the bar.

"Nice bracelet," he said, putting down his glass. "Listen. I can be whatever you want me to be. It's what I do. It's what I'm good at. Just remember that. You want me to be your best friend *and* fuck you? No problem. You want me to romance you, take you to dinner and shit? No problem." He took a drink. And added as an important afterthought, "Only thing I won't do is beat you up."

Now it has been my experience (after all, I am almost thirty-five years old and I know a little about these things), it has been my experience that when two people talk about sex, sex in the abstract, if there is such a thing, it is a way of fucking before you get into bed, trying it out, seeing if it's going to work. And it seemed to me that this is what Detective Malloy was doing, sitting there with his smile and his faggot hands and his eyes. Giving me a play. He was moving a little fast, but he'd put it right out there. He'd put it in my head. Or in my lap. Not that it wasn't there already.

"It mustn't be too easy living with your ex-wife," I said.

"What do you mean?" He looked surprised.

"Dating. Not beating up girls."

"You don't know any cops. I have friends who haven't been home in years." He looked at me. "Look, cops make the worst husbands. You know what I'm saying?"

"Sounds like they don't make such great boyfriends, either."

"Cops go through girlfriends like they go through veal cutlets."

I found myself wondering idly if he was the type who needed to talk about it after, maybe on the phone a couple of days later. The more polite ask if your vagina has retained its shape. Not too sore. Not stretched the size of Shea Stadium.

I suddenly didn't want to talk about girls. Or veal cutlets. "Why does your partner have a water pistol in his holster?"

"They took his gun away. He's still working. He's just not working with me tonight."

"You're working now?"

"Yeah. Shit, yeah. What'd you think we were doing? This is what's called a canvass. Right now. I'm questioning you. That it happens to be in a bar don't make no difference. Listen," he said with a weary sigh, "the bureau's changed a lot since I first come on the job. Being in Homicide now is really just EMS for dead people."

"Why is your partner on leave?"

"It's called restricted duty, not leave." He took a drink. "His wife caught him with another woman. A big fat chick. He likes fat girls."

"Infidelity is reason to take away a cop's gun?"

"His old lady ran outside and scratched her name with her keys on the hood of his new car. By the time he got outside, she was on the second n. Her name's Lonnie. L-O-N-N-I-E. He lost his temper and went after her and she ran inside the apartment and threw his Hispanic Society trophy out the window." He frowned. "And, ah, that's, you know, when he tried to kill her."

I didn't know what to say.

"Richie wishes he could be a dyke 'cause then he could just have sex with women and forget all the other shit. You know what I'm saying? Marriage and kids and shit. Mortgages. Only I tell him he wouldn't be too good at it."

"Why is that?"

"What some people call oral sex. Spanish guys, black guys don't like it. Richie says he won't eat nothing that gets up and walks away."

"I'm glad you told me," I said.

"Richie loved that trophy, man. It was for the San Juan Citizen of the Year or some shit. He takes that stuff seriously. It means a lot to him."

The story made me smile and I wondered if it made me smile because I wanted him to like me. I was a little worried when I realized that it was more than wanting him to like me. I realized that I wanted to be like him. "Yes," I said. "It is a good reason to kill your wife. I mean, of all the reasons I can think of." Wondering if I meant it. Worried that I meant it.

"They took his gun and his shield and put him on restricted duty. He's a housemouse now, filing papers. When they first questioned him downtown he asked if they wanted to see his official letter from the police shrink. He got it two years ago when his old lady called the chief of detectives and threatened to kill herself unless Rodriguez came home. They said, yeah, let's see the letter. He showed it to them and the fucking fat fucks confiscated it."

He began to laugh. He lifted his foot onto a rung of my barstool and I saw the black holster around his ankle. "They told him they'd give him back the letter when they returned his shield and his gun. So now he's got nothing. No wife, no gun, no shield, no note that says he's not nuts. The note's the worst part. He looked at that note every day, man."

"What are housemouses? Housemice, I mean."

"Housemouses."

"Housemouses."

"Guys who put their balls in a drawer. Guys who take promotion tests. Guys who don't want to be in the street. Guys who are lazy. Or scared."

He ordered another round, even though I had not finished my drink. The bartender took a ten-dollar bill from the change on top of the bar. Like most people who are anecdotal, he told me nothing. He revealed nothing about himself. He talked a lot, but he only told me what he wanted me to know. Which wasn't much.

"You sure we don't know each other?" he asked suddenly. "I swear to Christ I seen you somewhere before. You ever been down the shore? Maybe that's where I saw you. You wear a polka-dot bikini?"

I looked into those cold blue eyes. Something in me, some old, stubborn resistance-fighter tactic made me lie, made me say, "No, I don't. Know you." It would have been my third or sixth or tenth mistake. I'd stopped counting. "I just remind you of someone," I said.

"Yeah," he said, looking around. "That must be it."

There was a pretty black girl sitting at the bar, near the door, and when I looked up I saw that she was staring at him. I turned to see if he had noticed. I should have known better.

"You stare back at them," he said, leaning close to me. "That's how you flirt with black girls. But with white chicks, I myself like to look, get caught, look away. Five or six times is good. Then she thinks she's got you."

He looked at her again. "You want to pick her up?"

I looked at her, surprised that I was considering it, although it was not something I'd ever done, fuck a man and a woman at the same time. I realized with even more surprise that while it already seemed that I was interested in doing whatever it was this man wanted, I did not want to pick up another girl. I would be too jealous. I didn't want to share him.

"No," I said.

"Listen," he said quietly. "Just so's you know. There's not too much I haven't done."

Always an interesting move, I thought. Feeling my body flush. Boast disguised as confession. Threat disguised as confession.

"Ever fuck somebody dead?" I asked. I wasn't nearly as

good as he was, I knew, but I could at least try to stay in the game.

"Someone dead?" He laughed. "No. No one dead. No one that I *knew* was dead."

"That boy was with me tonight. The one you wanted to talk to." Changing the subject again.

He wiped his mouth. "I don't need to talk to nobody."

I was surprised.

"Not yet. Whoever did this one broad knows all about bodies. It's not easy to cut a throat like that. Your friend Cornelius isn't into popping arms out of sockets and ripping them from the body, is he?"

"Not that I know."

"You got to meat-cut it, like cutting up a chicken almost, you know what I'm saying? how you take the legs off a cooked chicken? Pop."

He took my arm and held it away from my side, putting a hand between my breast and my arm. I felt as if I'd been branded.

"The humerus here," he said. "And this joint at the shoulder. Very difficult. You got to know what you're doing."

Like you, I thought.

He suddenly smiled. And let go of my arm.

I looked over my shoulder, wondering what had distracted him.

Big handsome Detective Rodriguez who don't eat nothing that gets up and walks away.

"Hi," I said.

"Hi, how you doing?" He looked around the room.

"How'd you get out, man?" Malloy asked, his voice

changing from his talking-to-a-broad voice to his talking-to-a-man voice. "They let you out?"

Rodriguez grinned. "What the fuck, I'm not going to do nothing. What can I do?" He reached inside his coat and pulled the plastic pistol from his holster with the map of Puerto Rico and shot a thin spray of water into Malloy's face.

I handed Malloy my paper napkin and he wiped his face. It was a girl thing, handing him the napkin, and I regretted it.

"If loving you is wrong," Rodriguez said to Malloy, "I don't want to be right."

"No, you don't," said Malloy.

"I had to park on Christopher Street. There were a hundred fucking guys looking to have a couple hundred sexual encounters each." He shook his head in disgust.

"You wouldn't mind if some guy were trying to fuck a hundred women a night," I heard myself say.

"How'd you know?" he asked. He ordered a vodka and cranberry juice. For his cystitis. From sitting on top. I had a sudden dislike for him, which surprised me, given his great personal, or more precisely his great impersonal, beauty, a male characteristic I tend to value, and his very cool, very still, very uninterested manner, which I value even more.

He said to Malloy, "One of the civilian secretaries, you know her, Dewanne, the skinny broad, said to me today, 'What's the difference between sixty-nine and the police department?'" He looked at me. "You know this joke?"

I shook my head. "Not yet."

He turned back to Malloy. "In sixty-nine you only have to look at one asshole."

Malloy smiled. "She's a good kid. She writes out my messages three times."

"She wants to suck your dick," Rodriguez said. He looked around the room again, and he, too, saw the black girl. He smiled at her. Malloy caught me watching Rodriguez and winked at me.

"I thought you only liked dark meat on Thanksgiving," Malloy said to him. He ordered another round. "We know each other twenty years," Malloy said to me.

"Longer," said Rodriguez, not taking his eyes from the girl.

"Where's Marty?" Malloy asked him.

"He called in for a Twenty-eight. Said his mother was sick."

"There was a homicide in the Three-Four," Malloy said. "A ground ball. Some spic did his wife. The captain went up."

Rodriguez nodded. "She must not of known when to shut up."

I wondered if Rodriguez thought of himself as a spic.

Rodriguez looked away from the girl and said, "You know, all you really need is two tits, a hole and a heartbeat."

Malloy said mildly, "You don't really need the tits."

Rodriguez said, "You don't even need the heartbeat."

I reminded myself that Pauline says they have to despise us in order to come near us, in order to overcome their terrible fear of us. She has some very romantic ideas. I tried hard, but there must have been something a little pinched in my face, a momentary faltering, because Rodriguez said to me, "You're one of those broads, right? You know, man, one of those feminist broads." Working a lot of gender into one sentence.

"I was thinking you might be one, too," I said. "Detective Malloy told me you like fat women. And that made me think you had a generous, perhaps even sympathetic view of women."

To my surprise, he smiled, the irritation fading from his big handsome face. I was beginning to think he wasn't so good-looking after all.

"Did Detective Malloy tell you why?" he asked.

"I never got that far," Malloy said. He looked a little embarrassed.

"Fat chicks," Rodriguez said, "are always in a good mood when you call, even if it's late. They always say, come on over, I wasn't asleep. They cook for you. Even if it's five in the morning. They're cool." He nodded, pleased with himself.

I looked at him, wondering if thin girls made a practice of refusing to cook for cops. Maybe.

"You probably never been fat your whole life," he said to me.

Although I do not like anyone intervening on my behalf, especially a man, I would have been very happy if Malloy had told Rodriguez to go fuck himself. I looked around the bar. Almost everyone seemed to be dressed for traveling. Shorts. Flip-flops. Sweat suits made of crinkled parachute silk. Pauline has the best clothes-sighting on an airplane, having sat next to a man in a wet bathing suit on a flight from Miami to New York. Malloy and Rodriguez were the only men in suits. White shirts, ties. They even kept on their jackets.

Rodriguez looked at his watch. "I got to be getting back. I'm going fishing tomorrow."

"You really eat those things you catch?" Malloy asked. "They're in the *Hudson*, man."

"What's wrong with the Hudson? There's all kinds of shit in the Hudson."

Malloy laughed. "Well, don't drown." He pronounced it "drownd."

"You want me to sign you out?" Rodriguez asked him. I wondered if this was something he did for Malloy on a regular basis. Cover for him. Break the rules. What he was doing, I realized, was letting both Malloy and me know that he knew Malloy was trying to fuck me.

"No," Malloy said. "I'm leaving, too."

I felt myself blush with disappointment. I looked away, afraid that they would see it.

"Well, I'll catch you over there, man," Rodriguez said. "Catch you later." He turned to me with a small smile of triumph. "You come here often? I mean, it's your neighborhood, right? Your local."

"She hangs out in those real downtown places," Malloy said.

I wondered if he meant the Pussy Cat Lounge. My local.

"I'll drop you off," Malloy said to me.

"See you later, man," Rodriguez said, already moving through the crowd.

"Does he really fish in the river?"

Malloy watched him leave. "He goes to this place near the George Washington Bridge. There's a little lighthouse there. It's locked to the public, but he goes there."

"How does he get in?"

He smiled. "We're detectives." He picked up the money on the bar and counted it, leaving five dollars on the counter. "We can do anything we want."

On the way home, I noticed that he didn't drive the way

most men drive in New York. He was slow, deliberate, confident. One foot on the gas, one foot on the brake. He didn't honk his horn or call anyone an asshole. I wondered if he fucked that way.

I didn't find out until later, in bed, dreaming him through my nightgown.

I've begun to keep a dictionary in preparation for a paper on New York street slang. It is a fluid list as the words are sometimes in use for only a month or two, the meaning of the word varying in different parts of the city, signifying one thing in Brooklyn and something else in the Bronx. The words themselves—in their wit, exuberance, mistakenness and violence—are thrilling to me:

    virginia, n., vagina (as in "he penetrated her virginia with a hammer")
    belows, n., pl., bowels, intestines
    wig hat, n., wig
    freezerator, n., refrigerator
    yams, n., pl., legs
    gangster lean, n., the cool way to sit in the driver's seat of a car, leaning to the window side
    snapper, n., vagina
    gash-hound, n., someone who loves gash
    brasole, n., vagina (from the Sicilian? *bresaola?* cured meat?)
    to skeeve, v., to disgust, repel; also a *skeeve,* n., a disgusting person (from the Italian *schifoso?*)

55

to pinch, v., to get or have (as in "to pinch some
   conversation")
tenderhooks, n., tenterhooks (misusage)
besides himself, phr., beside himself (misusage)
dishonorable recharge, phr., dishonorable discharge
   (misusage)

Well. I don't know where to start. What to say. What to
think.

I don't believe in astrological charts or psychic readings or
harmonic convergences or that the Pyramids were built by
extraterrestrials, and I don't believe in reincarnation. At least
not for me. Perhaps Mike Tyson will come back as a snow
leopard, although a snow leopard would appear to be already
too evolved, seeming feminine and mysterious. (In trying to
teach both anthropomorphism and simile to my class, I asked
them to make a list of animals and their attributes. Wise as
an owl, strong as an ox. I then asked them to explain the
difference between the two. No difference, they said. Owls
really are wise.)

I don't believe in destiny, although I am sometimes
tempted by the freedom implied by inevitability, at least in
the *Appointment in Samarra* sense. Unfortunately, it is not
Death who is waiting to take my soul at Houston and Broadway, but the crosstown bus I do not see coming.

Which leads me to coincidence. I do not believe in coincidence when it is manifested in behavior. There are excep-
tions, of course, but I tend to the view that most behavior is
neither accidental nor haphazard. For example, when my old
boyfriend Curtis happens to stop by late at night when my

new friend Teddy is trying to make a modified sailor's knot on the panty hose wrapped around my wrists, I do not believe it is coincidental.

What I am trying to say is that I do not think that any of the things that have happened to me in the last two weeks are the result of chance. Cornelius's difficulties with his murder-scape, as he calls it. Detective Malloy coming to see me. Even the gift of the baby bracelet.

This morning there was a rubber hand, the nails painted red, the kind of thing you can buy around Halloween, actually all year round now, in the front hall under my mailbox.

It is possible that it was left for the elderly man on the top floor who has not left his apartment in the seven months that I have lived here. I have let in the anxious Haitian delivery boy from Gristede's many times, so I know that Mr. Seidman is alive and fond of Aunt Jemima pancakes and kosher knockwurst, even if I have never laid eyes on him.

It is possible that it was left for the young couple who live one floor above me who own an Italian restaurant in SoHo and whose comings and goings are so satisfyingly regular that I know that it is one-thirty in the morning by the sound of their step in the hall. They are in love. They have had only one quarrel in six months, which came to me by way of the fan vent in the bathroom. She works at the restaurant as a hostess. He was angry because she had lingered a little too long at the table of a movie director whose name I could not quite hear.

But I do not really think the hand was left for Mr. Seidman, even to chide him for his poor tipping habits. (Good word, chide.) And I do not think that it was left as a warning to the sweet-natured girl upstairs to keep her hands to herself.

I think it was left for me.

I suspect that one of the reasons that John Graham is my friend is my weakness for humorous incongruity, although I prefer my humorous incongruity in language—the placid, volatile, clumsy lace-maker, for example.

John was an actor before going back to school to study medicine (what I mean when I say incongruity—in this instance, the incongruity of category). He is interested in the ear. That is his larger, or perhaps I should say smaller, field of study.

He often accuses me of being a word casuist. Which could be taken for a good thing, provided you think, as I do, that casuism is a precise and decorous examination. But I know what he means. I taught him the word in the first place. I do possess a certain rigidity, a certain prudishness. I hate it in myself. I even divide words into good and bad.

John believes that revelation, in particular revelation of self, constitutes so high an interest as to be, as he would say, a personal code. He told Pauline within minutes of meeting her that he thought he had been molested when he was fourteen years old. He still does not understand why I minded. It was only once, he said, referring to the possible assault, rather than the frequency with which it comes up in conversation.

But there he was last night, standing on the stoop, yelling up at my window to let him inside.

I let him in.

The first thing he said was that I did not look well.

I thanked him.

"No, really," he said.

I told him that I didn't need convincing, if that is what he meant.

"You look all tense and tired. Like when you're writing. You're not writing another book, are you?"

"I'm fine. Just fine. Although sorry to disappoint you."

"You need a back rub," he said. "That's what you need." He moved behind me and put his two hands on my shoulders. "I could give you an anatomy lesson at the same time."

"Only if you promise to skip the ears."

"Really?" He leaned around me, a hesitant smile on his tanned face.

I pulled away from him. "Are doctors allowed to have suntans?"

"I was walking Skip in the park late last night, late for me," he said quickly, "because I get up early to watch those news shows in the morning, everything that's happened while I'm asleep, and I saw you come in. I was going to come over, but I know how you feel about Skip."

"I thought you went to the park in the afternoon," I said, closing my notebooks, moving them to conceal a half-eaten hard-boiled egg. The egg was too spinsterly-looking a snack, too lonely-seeming, and I did not want to be lectured about my diet. Or my loneliness.

I do not like anyone looking at my work or reading my students' papers. I was convinced for a while that John had a crush on my student Andrea after he read a series of poems she'd written about her first sexual experience with her boyfriend Manny called the Ying-Yang Sonnets, which I, having

difficulty giving her a grade, had foolishly left on my desk.
It is hard for me to grade my students' writing. I cannot
imagine a standard of measurement that would be appro-
priate. If Faulkner is an A, Andrea, in that case, is an F. I
cannot use their own work as a measure since there is not
enough of it to judge. It is, I've explained to Mr. Reilly, who
teaches English Literature, an exemplary instance of grading
for effort. Which is why I announce at the beginning of each
term that unless they fuck up really bad (what's fucking up
really bad? Cornelius had asked to much hilarity), I will give
each of them an A.

Mr. Reilly, of course, disapproves. He is not especially interested in what he calls the teaching process. He thinks
teaching is a job like any other, as opposed to a calling or a
dedication, and I agree with him. He does not bother to conceal his boredom whenever we are forced to talk about the
curriculum. Or curricula, as he quite correctly says. His interest is food. He tells me what he has just eaten and what
he is about to eat, his pockmarked face full of ecstasy as he
describes for me the perfect bacon, lettuce and tomato sandwich. He once ran down the hall to show me a passage in
the correspondence of Jane Austen in which she admits that
good apple pie was a considerable part of her domestic happiness. I would mind, I think, if it were a conventional pre-
tension, if he went on for twenty minutes about the perfect
leek remoulade. But as his taste runs to Johnnycake with
Ritz crackers and syllabubs of candied fruit in aluminum
ice cube trays—foods possessing a kind of sugar-based post-
modernism—I mind it less.

Mr. Reilly thinks that I am too easy on my students. His
wife told me so. She teaches art at a girls' school. I met her

at a school production of *Uncle Tom's Cabin* in which the roles of slaves were played by the Caucasian and Asian students and the parts of white southerners were taken by black students. At Mr. Reilly's request, she had given the Design Committee a few misleading tips on painting canvas scenery. She had come to the final performance and been mildly surprised, but not apologetic, to see the scrims drift suddenly to the stage, draping the actors in a web of dusty gauze. Mr. Reilly, she said to me as if in explanation, always refers to his students as his drops-in-the-ocean. That's where we differ, I said to her. I like my students.

She stood next to Reilly in the back of the auditorium after the performance, holding his arm tightly. I could see that he despised her. He despised her ceramic brooch. He despised her eagerness to be introduced to what she called his colleagues. When he went off to find Miss Wein, a nearly deranged biology professor, Mrs. Reilly told me that her husband worried that I was handling my students all wrong. Handling? I asked. In a matter of seconds I, too, had come to despise her. Too lenient, she whispered. Letting them come to my apartment. Easy grading. It was too bad, he'd told her. I was going to get into trouble.

I did not bother to explain myself. It would have taken months. Years.

Mr. Reilly returned with two paper napkins of tiny pastel marshmallows. One for himself, and one for me. There are some people, Pauline says, usually women, whom you can fuck only if you have permission to kill them immediately afterward. Mr. Reilly would qualify. Mrs. Reilly you couldn't fuck at all.

"Well, the dog was depressed again," John said. "It was

hot today, wasn't it?" He looked around my apartment. "I was wondering whose car that was last night." He, too, picked up one of my mother's jade pins, and balanced it on his palm. The plump pad where his thumb joins the rest of his hand to make the Mound of Venus is unusually strong. He exercises his hands with weights. He is fastidious. He brushes his dog's teeth. He removes the staples from magazines before recycling.

"Whose car what was?"

"You got out of."

I didn't answer.

He said, "You got out of a gray car that looked like it just came from Beirut. I don't get how people can ride around in a filthy car."

"Oh," I said. "That car. One of my students."

I have been telling a lot of lies lately. When I talked to Pauline, she asked what I'd been doing, had I met anyone? what was going on? I said, nothing. Keeping Malloy a secret.

"One of your students? One of your student's fathers, maybe."

I wondered why it should matter to him.

"Well," he said, suddenly animated. "I really dropped by to see if you wanted to go to the movies tomorrow. There's that movie about Canadian orphans and priests."

"Maybe," I said. I was suddenly exhausted. It was a curious feeling, an actual physical tiredness as if I'd spent the day slapping my man's shirts against stones in the river. Grinding flour for his tortillas.

"I'll call you," I said.

"You say that, but you never do."

"Well, I will." Promising myself that if someone ever said that he would call me and then did not, I would not complain.

He nodded and walked to the door. I opened it, and he said, "Skip says hi."

I smiled. Wanting to shove him into the hall with its red-flocked Victorian wallpaper, not able to comfort him, not wanting to comfort him.

"Well, ciao," he said.

"Goodnight," I said. And closed the door and locked it and sat in front of the empty fireplace and wondered if he, too, was following me.

I have many more words for the dictionary, a lot of them cop words now. (I find myself looking at cops on the street, in their cars, on horseback in the park. I walked past two young officers at the corner of Waverly and MacDougal where the men play chess, never any women playing, and I heard one cop ask the other, Do you use butter or margarine?) I never paid much attention to cops before, and if I did, I saw them as adversaries. Not unlike the way Detective Malloy sees women.

On the subway this afternoon, the man sitting across from me was sucking his thumb, his forefinger curled gracefully over the bridge of his nose. He smiled and, lifting one finger from his nose, pointed at me. Not enough meat on you bones yet, he said, and got off the train at Fifty-ninth Street.

There seem to be more synonyms for guns than vaginas on this list. For a change.

bis, biscuit, n., hand gun

jammie, n., gun (perhaps of inferior make? one that jams?)

Kron, n., gun (maker's name)

oo-wop, n., gun

to trap off, v., to plea-bargain

mongo, n., scrap-metal scavenger (Brooklyn word)

to cap, v., to shoot (as in "to bust a cap in his black ass")

bomb, n., drug package

spot, n., apartment used specifically to sell drugs

fugazi, adj., phony (from the Italian?)

props, n., proper respect

heave, n., hideout, place where you sleep

coop, n., hideout

hummer, n., sexual act of holding testicles in mouth and humming; also hum-job (Bronx word)

skins, n., sex from a female (as in "getting some skins from the pretties")

t'ain't, n., the space between the vagina and the anus (as in "t'ain't pussy and t'ain't asshole")

meow, n., expedition, usually to make trouble or to shoplift (Brooklyn word)

toasted, adj., burned-out (as in "he's been a detective too long; he's toasted")

I walked across the park last night. The linden trees are in bloom for that short time each year when they cause the city to smell like someplace else. Or rather to smell the way I imagine Baden-Baden smells.

Pauline and I had sushi and cold sake at Sushi Girl and then went to the Pussy Cat, sitting at our favorite table in the back, a little round black metal table whose top was so sticky that my elbows were glued to it momentarily when we first sat down. Pauline was wearing a Japanese happi coat in honor of dinner, over a 1950s elastic bathing suit, and high-heeled Lucite mules.

It was Tuesday, our regular night at the Pussy Cat. The other patrons tend to be a refreshing blend of downtown artists who think it's cool to be in a bar filled with truckers on their way back to New Jersey, and the truckers themselves, who look almost exactly as you'd imagine (and not bad, by the way). It is unusual to see two women together at the Pussy Cat. The topless waitresses now and then put down their trays to dance for the customers, so perhaps the gentlemen in the bar assume that Pauline and I are Lesbians. They don't bother us. Which is just fine with us. (One of the advantages of living downtown is that the whispers and leers one encounters in other parts of the city take on a different tone once you get below Fourteenth Street. There are very direct requests for specific acts to which one can answer yes or no with equal directness, no feelings hurt either way, or bitchy remarks about one's appearance, not as in "great ass," but as in "terrible scarf-tying, girl.")

Tabu works Tuesday night. She is from Rumania. Despite having been at the Pussy Cat only five months, she has already mastered the art of lifting paper money, preferably twenties, from the bar-top with her vagina. Perhaps it was my complimenting Tabu late one night (she had accrued about a hundred dollars by then, as far as I could figure) that led to friendship. She probably thinks we're dykes, too. She offered to teach me the vagina trick but I explained that I had trouble enough with sit-ups. She thought my eyeglasses were an asset, giving me a kind of sexy schoolteacher look. That's what she is, Pauline shouted.

Pauline, who claims completely disingenuously to fuck only married men because she prefers to be alone on the holidays, began scolding me the moment our drinks arrived. It upsets her that I wear clothes that she considers so loose-fitting as to be like clown suits, and it upsets her that I do not have a boyfriend. She claims to understand why she does not have one, but she thinks it is preposterous that I don't. Both my clothes and my solitary life being instances of my unwillingness to seek romance. In her heart of hearts, she worries that I am going to end up like Miss Burgess, only without Miss Gerrold.

"I don't want a boyfriend," I said. "I don't even want any more friends."

"What about a fuck?"

"That would be fine."

"Any of your students look promising?"

"A little young. Besides, I'm trying to convince them that self-expression in itself is not a criterion for anything. Well, maybe sex. Certainly not art."

"It's not?" She sounded disappointed. "I thought it was the only reason."

"No," I said.

"I've stopped seeing Mr. Kaplan," she said, looking around the bar. "Well, let's be honest, he stopped seeing me." She brought a shot glass of tequila to her mouth and threw back her head, drinking it in two gulps. Her eyes were suddenly full of tears, and I leaned across the table, squinting at her. "Don't," she said quickly. "It's just the tequila."

Pauline is organized. Massively organized, as she would

say. She has money now, thanks to her ability to anticipate what it is that the public will next decide is indispensable. It is Pauline who dreamed up coffee bars, and I am grateful to her. She just knows these things, she says, and I believe her. Unlike myself, she has the accident of style rather than the intention. No one in New York can open a restaurant without paying her a lot of money to tell them how to set up the tables. Her sexual swagger is only the convention of a woman who suspects that there is little hope for happiness with a man, and who hedges her bet by pretending that she is grateful to be alone.

"Have you noticed," I asked, "that grown men and women now refer to their fathers as 'my dad'?"

"I'm glad to see you're wearing the charm bracelet, even if your luck hasn't changed."

"How do you know my luck hasn't changed?"

"Your clothes. Your trousers have *pleats*."

"What's wrong with pleats?"

She waved her hand vaguely. "Too hard to explain."

"Mr. Kaplan doesn't deserve you. You didn't loan him money, did you?"

"No," she said. "It was my fault."

I waited for her to go on.

"Sexually," she said. "I was too aggressive."

I was immediately angry on her behalf. "Perhaps in the sense of frequency?" I asked.

"No, not that. More like, could you do this, no, thanks, not there, *there*."

I have noticed that if a woman can manage to tell a man what it is that she would like him to do to her body, the more accomplished the man believes himself to be, the more middle-aged he is, the harder it will be to get his attention. That is why it is so nice to sleep with a young man. You can say to him, Do this, sweetheart, now do that, and he's neither impatient nor offended nor intimidated. He's grateful. And obedient. The best lovers, Pauline and I agree, are men who have been seduced when they were boys by older women.

"What exactly was it that you wanted Mr. Kaplan to do?" I asked.

"I think it was, fuck me from behind."

"Oh. What an unreasonable request."

"You know," she said dreamily, "I can remember every man I ever fucked by the way he liked to do it. Not the way I liked to do it."

"Yes," I said with a loud, sympathetic sigh that made me think I might be drunk. I looked around the room. A man in a suit and tie at a table near the door was staring at us a little more than I'd come to expect in the Pussy Cat given the other, more obvious distractions in the room. I wondered if he was one of those men, of whom Pauline tells me there are many, who likes to watch two women make love.

"I think sometimes it's just me," she said. "Are other women able to say, Bend over the sofa, suck my dick, pinch my nipples?"

"Probably not suck my dick."

She raised an arm to order more drinks. "I'm paying to-night," she said.

"No, you paid last time."

"I have more money than you."

"Too bad."

"Did you ever fuck Mark Handlish in London?" she asked.

"No, you're thinking of Gavin Bromelly. We both slept with Gavin Bromelly. Mr. Thimble. Although not at the same time." I was suddenly depressed.

"I had him after you," she said. "You probably taught him that trick with the martini olives. Or did I? I can't remember. The only way I could tell he'd come was that he'd look at his watch." She took a drink of tequila. "I was sitting in a restaurant the other night. There were twelve people at the table and I knew that there was something odd, something eerily familiar, and by dessert I'd finally figured it out. I had slept with three of them. What was so upsetting was that it mattered so little. It counted for nothing. Nothing, I tell you. Not to me, not to them. It was terrible."

"Do you remember Tony Garr? He was at Cambridge when Anton was there. He used to insist that I wear all of my clothes in bed. I was inexperienced, I admit, but I knew that you were supposed to take off your clothes. It was so uncomfortable."

"Not to mention the laundry bill."

"I used to wonder what he would have done if I'd insisted he keep on all of his clothes. I mean, a blow-job is one thing. But in bed. And in those big manly clothes. The shoes."

"Do you think Gavin Bromelly really believed that fucking in the sink was a comfortable position?"

"Gavin used to fuck you in the sink?" I asked, a little hurt.

"Once," she said quickly. "Only once. When his wife was in Marbella."

"Oh," I said, mollified.

"Maybe one other time."

"Hey, babe," I said. "Love hurts."

"No," she said. "I thought of that. The mirror was the

point. He liked watching himself in the mirror when he came." She lit a cigarette. "How is it that you aren't addicted?"

"You're going to have to be more specific."

"You may drink too much now and then, but that doesn't count."

"It's because I've spent my entire life with old people. First my parents and then my husband."

"That doesn't rule out pills. Old people take pills."

"I was corrupted in other ways. I was led to believe that intelligence made a difference."

"Hi, ladies," said our waitress as she put four shot glasses of tequila on the table.

"Hi, Janey," we said.

"What's up?" she asked.

"Talking about hard-ons," Pauline said.

"Oh," she said, disappointed. She was wearing a thong, and white beaded Indian moccasins, the kind you can buy in airports.

"I didn't order all of these," Pauline said. "Although I might have."

"That guy over there said to send over doubles of whatever you gals wanted," Janey said, gesturing with her chin.

We looked behind her. There was no one there.

"What guy?" I asked.

She shrugged, already busy at another table, either trying to put a man's hand between her breasts or take it away, I couldn't tell. I watched her move gracefully around the tables, joking with the men.

"I'm going home," I said to Pauline.

"Yes," she said, "me, too."

She allowed me to pay half the bill and we kissed good-night and she went up the stairs to her apartment.

I stood on the street, smelling the diesel from the trucks on the West Side Highway and the odor of brine from the Hudson River, too faint to be really pleasing, and that particular New York smell, at least in summer, of urine.

It was not far to Washington Square, an easy walk, but as it was one o'clock in the morning, I decided to forgo my usual habit of walking up Broadway and walk along West Broadway instead. Broadway, although well lighted, would be deserted. At least West Broadway, despite the odd turn that it takes near Lispenard Street and three rat-stricken blocks, has a few restaurants that I knew would be open to light my way.

As I walked north, cars shooting past now and then like noisy comets, I decided that I would not mind excessively the seeing of a rat (Pauline once saw hundreds of them pour out of a Con Edison hole at the corner of Desbrosses and Hudson and undulate in ripples across the cobbled street and then undulate back again, diving into the hole as if the Pied Piper himself had summoned them back), but I would not be very happy to *hear* a rat. The sound fills me with particular dread. It is a high, beseeching call, like that of newly hatched birds, and it causes my hair to stand on end. I imagine that it causes the hair of most people to stand on end. I would almost rather a rat trot across my feet, as happened to a friend pushing her baby in a carriage in Central Park, a friend who not coincidentally left for Los Angeles the next morning, than *hear* a rat.

So I was on the lookout, if I can use that word in regard to listening, jingling my keys, swinging my arm so that the charm bracelet would sing its metallic song, giving any smart rat time to change his mind before leaping out of the vacant lot at the end of the block. Andrea, one of the more opinionated and thus more interesting students in class, once asked me why I had corrected the phrase "listened out of the corner of her ear" in one of her stories, and I had struggled for a few minutes, citing the mixed metaphor rule and other stylistic rigors, all the while thinking to myself that of course she was right to object. Fiction is just that. Well, I'd said, teasing her a little, if you can make it a magical ear, a Borges ear, perhaps you will convince me.

I walked along, having myself a time given the possibilities, given the fact that just that week a rubber hand had been left in my front hall. I had not mentioned it to Detective Malloy when I spoke to him on the phone. I could add it to a list of things that I seemed to be keeping from Detective Malloy. Questions that I was surprised I had not asked him. I wondered if he knew that I was the girl in the dark basement room. I wondered if, in some way that I did not understand, he was using that knowledge to presume an intimacy between us, as if we shared a secret that was exciting because it was dangerous to both of us: A woman with red hair had been on her knees with his red cock in her red mouth a few hours before having her throat cut and her arms and legs pulled from their sockets.

I walked north on West Broadway, a little drunk, harking for rats, wondering if he liked the way she sucked his cock, when I heard the sound of footsteps behind me, beneath the distant swish-sound of the trucks. I looked over my shoulder.

There was no one there. Which frightened me. Because I could hear him.

I was not far from Canal Street. There was a café on Canal that would be open. I would go inside. I had just enough money to order an espresso, New York waiters being difficult about women smelling of mescal rushing in from the street shouting that they are being followed. I smiled at myself. For a moment, I had even imagined that I could hear breathing.

There was the sudden sound of a car alarm and it made me jump. I looked behind me.

Clothed not in the black suit of an undertaker, not even black-skinned, but in some black and shiny material like plastic or, more terrifying, rubber, an arm wrapped casually, easily around my neck. My head was yanked back, my neck pulled taut, a hand over my gaping mouth.

He wore a black stocking mask, black holes for eyes. There was a strange odor on his gloves, like glue or acetone. Formaldehyde.

He moved me forward with his legs, my feet dragging on the ground. There was a car parked in the empty lot ahead and I realized that he was not going to kill me. Not kill me there on West Broadway. He was going to take me someplace else. And kill me.

I jammed my feet into the pavement and threw back my head, grabbing at the mask, convinced that if I could see him I would at least know that he existed, that he was not an incubus, a hoodoo sent from the depths or even from Samarra to take me away.

The keys were in my uplifted hand as I caught hold of the bottom of the mask. He pressed his chin deep into my shoulder. I dragged the keys across his neck, hurting him,

73

and in the instant of his startled recoil, he let go of me and I fell away from him, onto the pavement. A taxi rounded the little bend at Walker Street as I rolled into the street. The car stopped with a streak of brake and the stink of slopped gasoline, and veered onto the curb.

I looked behind me.

He was gone.

The driver, a nervous young Pakistani who thought that I wished to harm him in some way with his employer, his wife, the consul general, allowed me into the back of his car and took me home, promising the whole way that there would be no charge, no charge, the meter was off. Just for me. No charge.

I dialed his beeper number and he called me back five minutes later. I'll be right there, he said when I told him. Are you okay? I'm on my way.

I put on my glasses and ran downstairs and sat on the top stair of the stoop, leaning back against the front door, waiting for him, jumping up and then sitting down again, watching the last drug dealers walk round the corner of the park and back again, working late. This must be the shift they give the new men, I thought, drug dealing being a candidly hierarchical arrangement.

He was there in ten minutes. "I was near here," he said, coming quickly up the stairs.

He took me by the arm and helped me to my feet and we went inside.

"Near here?" I asked.

"That gambling club above the Red Turtle. The one a friend of mine owns," he said. "The ex-cop. I mentioned it to you once before."

I shook my head.

"You don't remember."

We went into the kitchen and I asked him what he wanted and he said, "Bourbon."

I gave him the drink and he sat down in the living room. My hands were trembling.

"That's good," he said, tasting it. Looking at me.

I walked back and forth.

"Tell me what happened," he said quietly.

I told him, grateful not to be scolded, trying to keep it simple the way one learns to do, not telling your doctor or your pharmacist or your police officer everything that has pained you in the last two years, and he listened without interruption, only stopping me to ask, had I seen the man's face? could I identify him? He asked me twice.

When I finished, he put down the drink and said, "It sounds like someone just trying to take your money. Take your purse. That's what it sounds like. What about your friend, what's her name, Pauline? Did she get a look at anyone?"

"She wasn't with me. She lives above the bar on Chapel Street."

"She lives alone?"

I nodded.

"On the second floor?"

"Third."

"Is she careful?"

"Careful?"

"More careful than you? I'm surprised only one guy tried to jump you. Walking on West Broadway."

"I do it all the time."

"Well, don't."

"Where was she killed?"

"Who?"

"That girl with the red hair. The girl who was killed in the Red Turtle."

"Who told you she had red hair?"

"Your friend."

"My friend?"

"The man with the water pistol."

"My partner. You mean my partner."

"He showed me a photograph. In the car that night when you questioned me."

It was suddenly difficult to breathe. I closed the windows and turned on the air conditioner.

"She wasn't killed in the bar," he said slowly. "You're confused."

I could see one of the drug dealers from the window, standing under the Hanging Elm, looking up at me. "What is disarticulation exactly?"

"I told you."

"Tell me again."

"It is when an arm or a leg is pulled out of the joint, not cut, not sawed, but pulled out. Probably with a foot placed on the shoulder or hip. For leverage. It makes a funny sound."

"That girl was killed that way?"

"No."

I waited for him to go on, but he was silent.

"How was she killed?" I asked.

"With a straight razor." He stopped. "It seems to me like maybe he was trying to take the head and something happened. Maybe he wasn't too good at the cutting part yet. He was trying to fit her into something. A bag, maybe. A box."

"The cutting part?"

"Somewhere between the fifth and sixth cervical vertebrae."

"And?"

"And what?"

"Is that all?"

He didn't answer.

"What else?" I turned to look at him. "You said there were two murders."

"Did I?" He ran his hand through his hair. "A disarticulated body, cut the same way, was found six months ago. Well, parts of a body. We don't know yet if it's connected to the DOA last week. They don't think so. Richie don't think so. But I think so." He stood up. "Why don't you come over here and sit down."

I shook my head.

"What was her name?"

"Whose name?"

"The girl in the Red Turtle. The DOA, as you call her. The girl with the red hair."

He was silent. Waiting. Then he said, "Angela Sands."

"And it was the same killer."

"We don't know yet." He spoke slowly, deliberately. "I personally think it's the same killer. But I can't prove it. Not yet. I can't even explain why I think it. Richie thinks I'm crazy. A dismembered female body was found last January along the river. She was wrapped in sections of the Sunday *Daily News*." He paused. "This happens all the time," he said. "You know what I'm saying?"

"What happens?"

"Murder."

I was silent.

"That's the thing about it. It never stops. Never."

"Why do you think it's the same killer?"

"Because something was taken from the bodies. Something was missing." He spoke reluctantly. "A souvenir. What's called a souvenir. The slashing is the same. He cuts a certain way."

Yes, I thought, I know that. The difference between male and female perversion. The action of the man is directed toward a symbol, not himself. The woman acts against herself.

"Souvenir? You mean, like a memento?"

"The killer gets to do it over again whenever he wants. You know. Fantasize. In private. Like jerking off."

"Like jerking off?"

"Jerking off."

I nodded. I was suddenly afraid that if I seemed too upset or afraid, too crazy, he would stop. "What did he take from her?"

"You really want to know this shit?" he asked, frowning.

"Someone," I said, "left a rubber hand under my mailbox."

"When was this?"

"Last week. Tuesday. Monday."

"Why didn't you tell me?"

"Does he take hands?"

He stood, the chair still startling him a little, even though he'd sat in it a few times by then. "Tell me again," he said.

"What happened to you tonight. Go over it once again. Come here. Show me."

He came up behind me and pulled me back against him, my head against his shoulder. I took his right arm, bending it at the elbow, and laid it across my neck. I could feel his breath against the side of my face.

Like this, I said. Like this.

He let his arm fall from my neck, down across my chest, until his hand was on my breast, his fingers finding the nipple. He pulled me back against him. He had an erection. I could feel it.

"All right," I said. "All right."

He followed me into the bedroom, taking off his clothes, having trouble for a moment unbuckling the ankle holster, laying the revolver on the mantelpiece.

I looked at him. He had a long scar down the right side of his stomach. He was high-waisted. Strong. Black hair on his shoulders. More than I like. He had no shamrock tattoo. In fact, he didn't have much of anything on his ass.

He lay on his back on the bed, hands folded behind his head, and watched me as if it were his habit. His due.

I took off my glasses. I took off my blue and white striped dress, watching myself through his calm, shrewd eyes, standing alongside the bed, still wearing underpants.

"Take those off," he said.

I shook my head.

He sat up quickly and pulled down my underpants, and with one hand at the small of my back pushed me face down on the bed while he put his other hand between my thighs, spreading me apart, opening my legs for his mouth.

He put his tongue inside of me, in my vagina, in my ass,

and then he lifted my hips and turned me so that I was on my back, my legs over the side of the bed, bent at the knee, and he kneeled on the floor, his fingers inside of me, too, hooked deep inside, the way a man carries something hooked on a finger over his shoulder, and he sucked my clitoris into his mouth.

There was nothing intervening. Not a nightgown. Not even a penis.

"Come all over me," he said.

Later when I couldn't sleep because I kept going over and over what had happened in the street, over and over in that way of time attenuated, slowed down and exaggerated, he said, "There's nothing to be afraid of."

"I was wondering about you," I said.

"Don't," he said.

"Don't you want to know?" I asked. "What I was wondering?"

He sighed in that way men do when they want to sleep, not angry, only exasperated, tolerant, even affectionate. As if it gave him a little pleasure to indulge me. "What?"

"What you did to me," I said.

"What I did to you?"

"I want to know how you did it to me," I said. "Just in case I don't see you again. So I can do it to myself."

"You'll see me again."

"Someone taught you. An older woman."

"Get the fuck out of here," he said, laughing. For the first time, he sounded shy.

"Tell me," I said. "It will make my head stop for a minute."

He was silent. I waited, not knowing if he was asleep, men having the ability to fall asleep even when the conversation is about themselves. And then he said, "The first time I ate a broad, it was the Chicken Lady."

"I thought so."

"Get the fuck out of here. You know the Chicken Lady?"

I lay very still, arms at my sides, afraid that he would stop if I moved.

"I was fifteen. I worked at Bill's Butcher Shop on St. Nicholas Avenue delivering chickens. Her husband was a teacher at the Hebrew school on Saturday afternoons. It was summertime. She invited me in. She gave me a drink of water. We talked a little. I was up against the sink, drinking the water, and she came over and stood in front of me and took hold of my dick. I just stood there. I was scared. Nervous. She said, does this feel good? She asked me if I'd ever been with a woman, never taking her hand off my dick. She took me into the bedroom and started to undress me, kissing my chest. I kept asking if she was sure her husband wasn't coming home. She went right down and started to blow me. She got up and took her clothes off and I thought how big she was. She had a great ass. She was womanly."

"Did you like it?" I asked. I realized that I was whispering.

"Like it?"

"That she was womanly."

"I came to like it, but I didn't like it in the beginning. She was a mother. I mean, she was probably only twenty-seven, twenty-six, but I didn't know anything. I laid on top of her and I screwed her. I'm sure I came quick. I gave her a good hump, but I knew even though she didn't say nothing that it wasn't like banging a girl. When you bang a girl, they're not too experienced either, they keep their clothes on, they're embarrassed. But with her I knew she wanted more. There were things I knew I didn't do right. Things left undone. When it was over I felt empty. It was the first time it wasn't about me. It was the first time I realized there could be something better. She never said a thing. She never got up. I got dressed and she laid there nude. She knew her body was beautiful. Wide hips, nice small breasts. They stood out by themselves. White soft skin. She was good. Dark hair, black hair. Tight wiry pubic hair from thigh to thigh. I had never seen so much hair. Like Spanish girls, thick and coarse. She made me come over to her and she kissed me. She said, did I want her to show me what women like. I said yes. It was hard to get my hand inside of her. She had a meaty, fat pussy. You had to go all the way down to the bottom of her snatch to get your finger in. It was so strange once you got your finger in, it was like sticking your finger in the ocean. If she was sitting on me, I used to think she pissed on me. Hot liquid on my balls. I swear she used to piss on me. She told me to hold women when they come, to hold them in your arms. She taught me how to unhook a bra with one hand. She said it would come in handy someday. She asked me if I'd ever kissed a woman down there, and I said no. I may have lied to her. I might have done Margaret White at Rock-away. I don't remember. I asked her if women liked to have their asses licked and she said yes. She asked me if men liked to have their asses licked and I said no, and she licked me, and yes, I liked it. She never put her clothes on. I thought that was the coolest thing. She put a robe on to take me to the door and she gave me two dollars which I thought was fucking unbelievable. A six-pack cost maybe a dollar-three, and she said you can buy some beer and you can keep a dollar for yourself. The second time, I told her I basted the chickens extra long. Something stupid like that. She got the best fucking chickens in New York. What a dickhead I was. I'd clip the chicken snatches closed with little metal clips and baste them all morning. The second time I saw her I was more nervous. I thought about her all week long. I walked past her house. I looked for her on the street. She grabbed me and kissed me and told me she missed me. She told me I was a natural kisser. She laid on the bed without clothes on and we kissed for a long time. We only had forty-five minutes. She'd walk around, ask me if I wanted a soda, stand in front of me, her hands on her hips. I never saw her disheveled, or angry. The one thing she didn't teach me because I was always in a rush was to stick around. I was always getting laid on the run. Later, too, when I was a cop. Always on the fucking run. I told my friend Bozo about her and he didn't believe me so I took him to Fort Washington Avenue and we waited for her to come out, and she come out with a baby carriage. Oh, God. She said hi to me, very friendly, and I introduced her to Bozo. He still didn't believe I was fucking her. It went on for a year and a half, every Saturday. Years later, actually a couple years ago, I asked the other guys who were delivery kids at Bill's—the guy before me and the guy who came after me—I asked them both if she'd ever come on to them. And they said, no, as a matter of fact, she was a shit tipper. It made me feel good. I came one Saturday and she told me they were moving. She was upset, but I wasn't smart enough to know it then. She gave me thirty dollars and told me I would be a good man. Now go, she said. She kept saying, go. I'd always get halfway down the hallway and she'd call me back, saying Jimmy, Jimmy, come back, and she'd kiss me. The day I saw her the last time, she didn't call me back."

We were silent, both of us thinking.

"You know, she'd be sixty years old now. Jesus. Fuck me. Her son is thirty-two years old now. Fuck me. How cool is this. He's thirty-two."

"What was her name?"

"Annette, I think. I'm not sure. Annette."

"I'm in her debt."

He laughed. "Yeah. Well. We'll see."

He sat up, his stomach tucked in a fold, accommodating itself to his scar. "She reminds me of you a little," he said. "I mean, you remind me of her. Small back. Nice hips. Only her tits were small. She had great tits. Once when she was pregnant, I fucked her from behind on the bed on her hands and knees and I saw it in the mirror. It was weird, stomach hanging down, tits hanging down. I asked her if I'd made her pregnant and she just laughed."

"It must have been like sleeping with a goddess," I said.

"Yeah, she was gorgeous."

"I mean in another sense, too. In a mythic sense. In a ritual sense. It must have made you feel powerful. And powerless."

"Get the fuck out of here," he said. "Powerless?"

"Yes."

"*No.* Why would I feel powerless? How do you get me into these fucking conversations? You think too fucking much. It wasn't no myth."

I reached across his hip to touch his scar. He leaned away from me, pushing aside my hand. "I don't like it," he said. "If you touch it."

"I'm sorry," I said.

"You didn't do nothing," he said in surprise.

"I can be sorry even if it's not my fault."

He looked at me as if this were a new idea for him. He rubbed a red mark on his throat. "Look what you did," he said.

"I did not," I said, surprised.

"You don't remember? It was that good?"

I reached up and touched the red scratch across his throat. He pulled away and turned on the light to look at his watch, a gold Rolex, then turned it off again. It was three o'clock.

"I got to go," he said. "Mr. Sweeney the plumber's coming at nine. She works. I got to be up."

He was anxious to go, reluctant to go. Ready to go. "Who gave you that little ring?" I asked.

He looked at it. "My wife," he said.

"Your ex-wife."

"Yeah, my ex-wife."

"Does it matter?"

"What?"

"What time you come home?"

He wound the watch. "Mr. Sweeney might mind," he said, "but she don't care. She'll be asleep."

"Good," I said.

He looked at me, suddenly wary.

I put my hand in his lap and lifted his cock from his thigh.

He took my hand away and laid it across my stomach, patting my hand. "I'll never get out of here if you start," he said.

I didn't like that he had patted my hand. I sat up, my legs under me, and leaned back on my heels in that way that makes me think of the collection of pornography I once discovered in my father's library, in particular a print of a geisha with the heel of her bare foot in her vagina. Something I have never mastered. Something I've never even tried to master. I leaned over and drew him into my mouth.

He resisted for a moment, laughing, nudging aside my head with his hip, and then with a heavy sigh, as if I were leading him to his doom, he leaned back on the bed, elbows bent, and watched me.

He was soft, tasting like salt. He got hard very fast, and I realized that I was moving my head in the same slow dipping way that the girl with the red hair had moved her head, wondering if he had taught her, knowing that he would have liked it a certain way, just the lips, not too hard, slower, a finger in his ass, no hands, no time, all the time in the world.

He reached behind and pulled a pillow under his head, settling in. He put one hand between my knees, between my legs, between my ankles, and pulled hard on me, the labia in his closed fist, swollen, loose, open.

He sat up and put an arm around my waist, turning me over and pulling me toward him so that I was on my knees, my ass high against him, his hand at the small of my back, holding me to the bed. My face pressed into the bed. My arms stretched above my head. He pulled my arms to him and took my two hands and placed them on my ass, and then with his hands on top of mine, he pulled me open, apart, exposed to him with my own hands, arched, spanned, and with a low moan he entered me with such ease, such presumption, that I began to come the moment he was inside of me. He said, "That's right, that's right." He ran his hand down my back, reaching beneath me to lift my swaying breasts, running his thumb between my buttocks, stopping for a moment at my opening, wetting it from my vagina, teasing, threatening. Then he let himself slide out of me and I turned on my side, hands between my legs in some girlish prolongment of pleasure, and he put himself roughly in my mouth, and I forgot about the girl with the red hair, the dead red girl. Opening my mouth, his balls in my hand, tracing with my finger the soft fluted ridge between anus and penis, back and forth, wetting it with my tongue, and then in that gesture I had seen him use once before, he put both hands on my head, slowing me down a little, keeping me steady, letting me know, and with a small shudder, a tender arch of back, he came in my mouth.

His orgasm was short, doubled and tripled with a quick convulsion, so private, so disciplined that he made no cry, no whisper, no exhortation. In case the Chicken Lady's husband walked in unexpectedly, his yarmulke held in place with two black bobby pins.

I am interested in The After. It is an expression I learned from Pauline, although it is not an idea I had to learn from anyone, being a woman, being left more often than not dangling precariously from a limb while he bounced to his feet, invigorated, refreshed, to pull on his pants (provided he'd taken them off). It seems to me that there is no underestimating the power of the male orgasm. With it comes not only satiation but a turning-away, an often friendly, sometimes even grateful turning-away in which he may even acknowledge, if only for a few minutes, that he is in the woman's debt. I once read that the female gorilla can—not *can* (because that implies potential), *does*—come up to fifty times in a single—what is the word? encounter? flirtation? pick-up? I think I will use mating. Which has caused me to think quite a bit about the whole thing.

So I was curious as to what the detective would do, wondering if he could keep it going at the high level of expertise he had already demonstrated. Unlike my students, Detective Malloy was all technique. Maybe too much technique. He had my permission to spell motherfucker any way he wanted.

He slipped away immediately in that careful, self-protecting way in which a man resumes the guardianship, the custodianship of his own penis. A reclaiming of the prize which only moments earlier he had given every sign of abandoning, squandering, even harming if need be, in the pursuit of satiety. He lifted himself heavily from the bed and went into the bathroom and washed himself in the sink. I listened to the water run for a long time and I wondered if he was using the pink nail brush in the shape of a duck. No, I decided, it would hurt. The penis after sex is particularly delicate, as any woman knows who has tried, even with the most innocent of intentions, to kiss it lightly or to lick it, curious perhaps about the taste and smell of herself who has been led to believe that she is capable of smelling unpleasant.

He came back to the bed, smelling of stephanotis soap, sighing as if he regretted leaving, although I thought not, that sudden oncoming of emptiness and sadness washing over me then, too. The desire for separation. I wanted to be alone in my bed, and he wanted to be gone, and neither of us minded, eager now for dissolution, not union. I was sleepy. And although I wanted to think about him, it would have to wait until the next day, perhaps until I was on the subway, where I seem to have most of my more interesting thoughts, listening to women talk about men.

He yawned and rubbed his hands over his chest and stomach. I lay back and watched him, arms behind my head, curious to see if the performance of his dressing would make me want him again. I didn't see why not.

Turquoise blue jockey shorts, a little faded, too many washings in Rockland County, balls lifted tenderly and placed with a little hitch of the hand, black socks, white shirt. No need for the yellow-striped tie. He held the tie aloft to even the ends, folded it neatly, shook it out again, not satisfied, refolded it and slid it carefully into the pocket of his jacket. He lifted one foot to rest it on the arm of a chair to tie his laces. He took the gun from the mantel and put it inside a black leather ankle holster that did not have a map of Ireland on it and slid it around his ankle, buckling it. All of this done quickly, smoothly, without self-consciousness even though he knew that I was watching him. I pretended not to be too interested in the gun. He pulled down his cuffs.

I didn't want to think of the number of women lying naked on beds, hands behind their heads, who'd watched him dress. He had done it a thousand times. Ten thousand times. And there was still pleasure in it. A man who knew he could fuck. Getting dressed. The woman watching from bed. Leaving before morning. He believed, I could see, in the principle of deferral. Like most men. Bafflement, distance, absence. Action driven forward by will, not understanding. It was this that made him dangerous. Not the sex. The deferral of consciousness. The deferral of meaning. And with it, despite the gift of the Chicken Lady given him by some generous guardian spirit, surely not St. Patrick, was the old brooding effacement of the female.

"I feel like I should be going to work," he said easily. "Only I'm going home. When you're home," he said, "getting ready to go in to work, it's like it's Friday night. It's always Friday night for a cop, even if it's Friday. You know what I'm saying? Maybe you got a date in the city. You're going to get laid. A stranger, someone new, 'cause you wouldn't take the trouble for someone you already fucked. Maybe it's been a particularly bad couple a days at home. She's pissed at you. But you feel good 'cause you're going in. You know the kids are going to be there all weekend, and you're not going to be there. It's a great feeling. You crack your shirt—a nice white shirt. The tie matches the shirt. Nice shoes. The suit fits well. You look sharp, you look clean. I used to think, what other job in the world is as good as being a detective? Your wife thinks you're going into the mouth of the lion and you're going in to get your dick sucked."

He dusted his hands. "You center your tie so you don't have that stupid piece of shit on the side. Maybe you even got a Windsor knot. The tie ends right where it's supposed to, on the belt buckle. You look in the mirror. You put on your cologne, slap your cheeks, shake out the trouser leg to cover your ankle holster. The fucking cat comes by, you kick it so it don't get no hairs on you. You take off your jacket, you say, what do you think, hon, you like this tie? I look okay today? She says, you look handsome, you look good. I ain't too fat? it's not too tight? You sit down at the kitchen table. Your jacket's folded on another chair. You tuck your tie in, you pull up your trousers 'cause of your creases, and you say, so what are you doing tomorrow, babe? She says, not much, ice-skating lessons, the mall. She asks, you be home tonight? You say, I don't know, what the fuck, it's

Friday night. All those n*****. I'll call you. If you wake up in the morning and I'm not there, don't worry. So she makes you a cup of International instant coffee, and you complain about the job. You got to complain. To make it look good. Friday night and every man in America is headed in the opposite direction. He's headed home, and you're going out. If you're a cop you're always moving in the opposite direction of everyone else. Someone screams fire, you run into the building." He sat on the edge of the bed, nudging my legs aside.

"Why did she kick you out?"

"Kick me out?"

I could see that he was offended, even if she had kicked him out. "Why were you divorced?" I asked, putting it another way.

"What do you want to know this shit for?" He sighed. "I dialed the same number twice."

"The same number?"

"Yeah. The first time I said, I'm doing overtime, I won't be home. The second time I said, take your clothes off, I'm coming over."

"Oh," I said.

"Yeah," he said.

"Why did you go back?"

"My kids. It was all fucked up. I missed my kids."

"Your kids? I didn't know you had children."

"Kevin was flunking out of school, the younger one never came home. She was working. She couldn't handle them. She had a boyfriend, some guy down at Central Booking. I'm not sure. Someone told me she did. But it wasn't that. To tell you the truth, I went home because I was tired."

"I didn't know you had kids," I said again.

"No," he said, without any sense that it was something I should have known. "Why would you know?"

"I wouldn't," I said. "I don't know anything about you."

"I thought I told you," he said coolly.

He wished to remain elusive even to himself. He was full of contradiction—penitential confessional eagerness and a secrecy that kept him opaque and in motion.

"My oldest kid wants to be a teacher," he said. "I don't know what the fuck happened to him. It's like Martians landed and took over his brain."

"What does he want to teach?"

"Schmoogs."

"Schmoogs?"

"Black kids. Can you fucking believe it?"

I was silent.

He smiled. "You think I'm a racist, like all cops." He didn't seem to mind. "Do you know how many of them have died in my arms?" He was suddenly angry. "You know, someday I'll get killed for one of them, not *by* one, *for* one." He looked away in disgust, whether disgust for me or them I couldn't tell.

"You're confusing what you do with what you think. Courage and prejudice," I said. "You're a professional. That's what you're supposed to do."

"I'm not confusing dick."

He was suddenly uneasy, as if he'd just begun to think about me, the kind of person I might be, the way that I might think.

"What is it exactly that I'm allowed to do with you?" I asked.

"Anything you want." He looked at his watch.

"Where do you live?"

"I told you."

"No, I mean the name. The name of the place. So I know where to imagine you." I had been thinking of the drive ahead of him, not of stopping by for tea with Mrs. Malloy, but it was too late to explain.

He tucked the sheet under my thigh. "You don't need to know," he said. "Where'd you get that bracelet?"

I looked at the bracelet, turning it, holding the gold bulb-baster in two fingers. The baby carriage charm was missing.

"One of the charms has fallen off," I said in surprise. I was upset to have lost it, feeling that it was some betrayal of the awful trust I'd inherited from Pauline's promiscuous aunt. "Maybe on the street. Maybe on West Broadway." I looked under the pillows and threw back the sheet. It wasn't there. I looked on the floor.

"That's too bad," he said. He went into the bathroom and combed his hair in the mirror.

I sat on the edge of the bed. "There's something I want to tell you," I said suddenly.

He looked at me as if I'd broken a promise. "What now?"

"You do know me," I said.

He turned back to the mirror. "What the fuck you talking about now?"

"Not know me. You've seen me."

He ran the comb under the faucet and shook it dry.

"At the Red Turtle. I saw you."

"All this time, I've been thinking, I know this fucking broad, I *know* her. And you're telling me I met you in the

Red Turtle? I don't think so, babe." He came across the room to get his jacket.

"It was dark. I was wearing my glasses."

"I think I'd remember those tits," he said, flicking my nipple with his finger. "I never seen you before in my life."

I nodded, knowing I'd gone far enough. Forcing myself to succumb to what was unconvincing. He wouldn't tell me. I wanted to ask if she was a good blow-job. I wanted to ask if he'd killed her. I was ashamed of myself for even thinking it. So ashamed of myself that I didn't tell him that I had seen his tattoo.

"You talk all the fuck over the place," he said. "You were going to show me the hand. Where is it?"

"Behind those books. I put it there so I wouldn't see it."

He found it and held it under the light. It was made of a hard white epoxy, not flexible, not hollow like a glove.

He reached across and ran the stiff fingers across my breasts. To my surprise, my nipples became hard. He didn't notice. I realized that I wanted him to make love to me again.

"I want to keep it," he said abruptly, slipping the hand into his pocket. "Maybe I can do something with it."

"Do something with it?"

The tips of the nails emerged from the top of his pocket.

"Lock the door after me," he said.

I nodded. "You never told me about the mementos," I said.

"Mementos?"

"What the killer takes."

"Souvenirs. Not mementos. Go to the door," he said. "I want to look at you." He took my hand and helped me from the bed and stood there, one hand on his hip, inside his open jacket, and watched me walk naked across the room. I was the Chicken Lady. He was the dazed initiate, fifteen years old, watching her walk to the door and open it for him.

I felt myself blush with desire. All the old credulities.

"I want more," I heard him say behind me. He stood by the bed, looking at me. "You wouldn't want the life of a cop," he said.

"I don't have to have the life of a cop."

He looked puzzled.

"I have my own life."

"Sorry. How Washington Heights of me."

"I'll be here," I said. I shuddered, perhaps from a draft.

"I know," he said.

And he left.

He telephoned this afternoon. There was a lot of noise in the background, and music, and a woman shouting.

"I'd like you to come in and look at some pictures," he said. "Could you do that?"

"I didn't see his face," I said. "I told you that."

"Well, just to make sure, you know what I'm saying? Just to be a hundred percent. You never know."

"I wish there were a way to do smells. I remember his smell every now and then."

"His smell?"

"There was a very particular smell. Like a dentist-smell. Or a stamp-collecting smell. Like glue."

He laughed. I heard a man yell, "Hey, Malloy."

"It's like trying to remember a dream," I said. "It's in me somewhere."

"I wish I were in you somewhere," he said.

To my surprise, I was a little disappointed. Too easy, I thought. "Where are you instead?"

"Working," he said. "I'll be here late. What about tomorrow night?"

I didn't know what he was asking. I didn't want to sound too easy myself. "Tomorrow night?" I asked.

"It's easier at night. Quieter. Not so many slappies. You could come in the evening if that's convenient. Richie's not too fucking happy working at the desk but I got him to start pulling pictures. He's mad at me anyways. We had a homicide on Bank Street the other night, a gay chap, and I took the deceased's Rolodex from the scene when I left. He must of had a thousand fucking names in it. All guys. I slipped in one of Richie's cards. You know, Detective Richard—only it should be Ricardo—Rodriguez. Only I wrote *un hombre magnífico* on the back of it, and *muy grande*. The detective who caught the case, a young guy, newwent through the file like he's supposed to and come across Richie's card. I was watching from across the room. I knew he found it 'cause he got all white. Which is hard to do if you're a n✻✻✻✻✻."

I am sorry to say that he made me laugh.

"He come across the squad room and showed it to me. What the fuck. He was whispering and shit. I said, You got to do it, man. Give Rodriguez a chance to explain, man. It don't mean he's a killer. I had to leave. I was afraid I'd give it up. The last thing I heard, Rodriguez was trying to throw the kid out the window."

"He is *un hombre magnífico*," I said.

He was silent. "You think so?" he asked at last. "Maybe for a Puerto Rican. Tall for a Spanish guy. He wants to take a ballet class. Says it's a great way to get laid."

I could hear Willie Nelson in the background. Perhaps Malloy wasn't at work.

"I wouldn't think it would be too hard for Detective Rodriguez to get laid." Making trouble. Smiling to myself.

"We were undercovers in Narcotics together. When we were still kids. He wasn't so tall then. I used to say Rodriguez almost always gets his man. Which is saying a lot."

"The other day you asked me why I was a cop. I've been thinking about it. I was drunk. I'd been drinking all night in a bar on St. Nicholas Avenue. I was twenty-two, just out of the Army, doing Dilaudid and a bottle of Robitussin every four hours. It seemed like a good idea." He paused again. "You ask a lot of questions."

"Do you want to go to the movies Wednesday night?"

He didn't even think about it. "I can't," he said. "I'm working. I'm trying to get on the log."

"The log?"

"Whenever you get overtime, they put you on the log. It's called the eternal log. Like the yule log. I always say: it's three o'clock in the afternoon, we get off in an hour, if we find two dead rabbis with broomsticks up their ass and their genitals in their mouth, we'll be working forever. If we find two Spanish guys, they'll send us home. So maybe I'll get lucky."

"Well, perhaps sometime when you're not taking rabbis' balls out of their mouths."

"Yeah," he said. "Maybe."

"Well, you let me know," I said. "When you're free."
Furious.

"What are you doing right now?" he asked, lowering his voice. It was hard to hear him.

"Standing at the kitchen window. Watching a man urinate in the street."

When I did not say anything more, he said, "Put your hand there. Cup it, weigh it." He waited. "The pussy that I like, when you slip your middle finger in, it's deep, and the folds of the vagina are floppy and soaking wet. You run your middle finger up. There's no greater feeling in the world than pussy like that. Your clit is right there. It comes down to meet me. It jumps in my hand. When you touch a woman and her clit is right out there, you know that she knows about sex. You know you can get to her. Like you."

"You can't get to me," I said.

"Put your hand between your legs," he said.

I did.

"Did you do it?"

"No."

"Put it inside your underwear."

I did.

"Inside."

I did.

"See how it jumps into your hand?"

I did.

Later, on the subway, I heard a woman say to another woman, That man, he a trisexual.

There was a small article in the *Times* Metro section today about the murder of Ms. Angela Sands, twenty-six years old, of Albany, New York, an actress who was an understudy in *The Will Rogers Follies*. There were no details of the murder. No mention of disarticulation. Or blow-jobs. (I could use a blow-job, he said this afternoon on the phone. Sometimes in the middle of it, he said, if you got someone knows what she's doing, she can slip one ball in her mouth. But you got to be careful. You don't want no amateurs around your nuts.) The newspaper did quote an anonymous police spokesman who called it a "grizzly murder."

I have new words for the dictionary.

> *to knock boots,* phr., to have sexual intercourse
> *track,* n., contract (as in "I got a track to kill him")
> *to do,* v., to fuck
> *to do,* v., to kill
> *clean,* adj., handsome
> *to Brodie,* v., to jump, usually from a building or a bridge; taken from a Mr. Brodie who claimed to have jumped off the Brooklyn Bridge
> *to lash,* v., to urinate
> *chronic,* n., marijuana, esp. high-quality
> *smudge,* n., black person
> *Ape Avenue,* n., Eighth Avenue (police slang)
> *puppy,* n., handgun (Jamaican word)
> *scrambler,* n., low-level runner for a drug dealer
> *cocola,* n., black person (Puerto Rican word)
> *spliv,* n., black person
> *to be hung like a horse,* phr., to have influential con-

nections in the police department; also a guy who is
hung like a horse

ground ball, phr., something easy or simple

to pull a train, v., to have group sex, gang-bang

slinger, n., drug dealer

to inflash, v., to inform (as in "he inflash me with the
bitch's scenario")

to double, v., to double-park

to sleep in a tent, exp., to have a large penis

to be built like a tripod, phr., to have a large penis

dixie cup, n., a person who is considered disposable

her, she, pron., wife

Cornelius came to me after class today. He had finished
a rough draft of his term paper and wanted to know if I
would look at it. He was still having a hard time with it, he
said.

I would have stayed after school to help him, but I was
meeting Mr. Reilly and Pauline at a restaurant Reilly had
been wanting to take me to called the Snack 'n' Chat. Pauline, who thought that the world was about to see a diner
renaissance, had asked to come along.

I invited Cornelius to come, too.

He hesitated. "What time you going?"

"Now," I said. "With my friend Pauline and Mr.
Reilly."

"Mr. Reilly?"

The students call Reilly "Ax" because of the humiliation
they suffer at his insistence that they speak correct American,
as he calls it. As in "ask." As if the way that Cornelius speaks

is not correct American. I *prefer* the way that Cornelius speaks. I wonder whether I should tell Cornelius that ax, as in ask, appears in Chaucer. And Faulkner.

"The restaurant's near here," I said. "I'll look at your paper while they talk about Formica tables. Come on."

I nudged him out the classroom door, wondering for a moment if I might be putting myself in a false position.

Yesterday he told me he didn't want me to take the subway, even during the day. He disapproves that I allow just anyone to come into my building. On the way to the restaurant, he was rude to a man who asked me for money. Cornelius mumbled a threatening incantation that included the word n*****, which worked in dissuading the man, but which made me feel embarrassed. Cornelius is heartless, not suffering the dispossessed, not believing them to be dispossessed, seeing most things in life as plays. Not unlike Detective Malloy. Secretive, wary, heartless. I wonder if Cornelius has a Jamaican flag on his ass.

What I had not considered until we got to the restaurant and I saw in Pauline's face a glimmer of sexual approval was that I might have put *him* in a false position. Pauline seemed to think Cornelius and I were on a date. His interest in me wasn't anything more than a hustle—for a good grade, for friendship, for relief from the boredom of school. Not for a fuck.

So I was not prepared, even if I should have been, when, sitting in a Naugahyde booth across from Pauline and Mr. Reilly, who really were talking about Formica, he pressed his leg against mine.

I moved closer to the wall.

"You all going to pass me, Mr. Reilly?" he asked.

Reilly looked up from the plastic bear filled with honey that he was turning over in his pink hands. "I don't see why I should," he said with a smile.

"Because you're sick of me," Cornelius said.

Reilly handed him a menu. "I'm sick of all of you," he said mildly.

Cornelius looked at me. "That means I'm getting an A. Now that I know the difference between ain't and aren't and shit." He pronounced the word "aren't" as if he had trouble getting it out of his mouth.

"What *is* the difference between aren't and shit?" Pauline asked, and I realized that she was flirting with him. It surprised me.

He ignored her, turning the full light of his charm—a charm she had instinctively recognized in the three minutes she'd been in his presence—onto me. Sitting next to him, pressed against the moose painting on the wall so as not to mislead him. He allied himself with me. Against her. Not that I had in any way indicated that I wished him to choose me.

My belated recognition of his desire actually served the purpose of provoking me to consider him, if only for a moment. It was like high school when just to hear that a boy liked you was sufficient encouragement to agree to go steady with him by the end of the day. Now that I think of it, it is just like life. Not high school.

The waitress, dressed in a pink uniform and white apron, came to the table and Pauline ordered the combination meat loaf and mashed potato dinner. Mr. Reilly ordered something called Thanksgiving on a Roll. I was scolded for ordering a tuna sandwich on whole wheat. Cornelius didn't order anything.

"I don't want no gravy and shit on my term paper," he said.

The waitress brought the food. Mr. Reilly's dinner looked delicious. It really was Thanksgiving on a roll. I don't know why I doubted it would be—two slices of white bread piled with stuffing, cranberry sauce, candied yams and gravy topped with a breast of turkey and two wings. I didn't want to watch him eat it. I'd once eaten crabs with him at a restaurant at the South Street Seaport and I haven't eaten crabs since. I don't begrudge erotic pleasure, whatever its source. I don't even begrudge Reilly his crunching and chewing and slicing and gnawing, but I didn't want to watch it.

"I'm booking, man," Cornelius said abruptly. Before I could say anything, he was in the street.

Reilly frowned at me, wiping his hands delicately on his napkin. "Never a good idea," he said.

"What's that?" I asked, knowing very well what he was going to say.

"Mingling," he said. "It makes a mess of things." He picked up a wing of the turkey and sucked the joint.

"Oh," I said, furious. "That argument. Too bad there isn't a Kentucky Fried Chicken nearby."

"There is," he said, lifting a tiny stem of a cranberry from the rim of his platter and flicking it to the table. "On Fourteenth Street."

"Would you like to try some of my meat loaf?" Pauline asked him. He would.

No wonder she ends up with marks on her ass from the sink, I thought. I ate the tuna fish sandwich that was so conventional that I began to feel sorry for it, so sorry for it that I ate it all, even eating what one of my students calls the garnage. We divided the check evenly and Reilly and Pauline made a date to go to the new restaurant in Chelsea where the waiters wear gaucho chaps and hats with dangling felt balls.

We left Mr. Reilly at his car and Pauline walked with me as far as Waverly Place, where we kissed goodbye.

As I walked home, I thought about the new poem in the Number Four subway. I have become so paranoid in the last month that I believe that the Poetry in Motion placards are messages for me. Not in a metaphorical sense, but literally selected for me by someone who has managed to gain influence over the Transit Authority Selection Committee. The new poem is a haiku by Yosano Akiko. "Come at last to this point/I look back on my passion/And realize that I/Have been like a blind man/Who is unafraid of the dark." For me, right?

My watch was broken, and while I knew that it was evening, I did not know the time. Not that it mattered. It is one of the things I learned in childhood—how to tell time without a watch. A sky, however, is needed. As I never actually see any source of light in New York, it is not easy to do here. Another thing I know from childhood is that the worms that cover the Philippine countryside work their way into your body through the soles of your feet and travel directly to your brain and eat it. These small but essential pieces of information were taught to me by Augustina, the woman who looked after me. I think of her often, perhaps because another invaluable thing that she taught me was to douche as a preventive against pregnancy with a clotted concoction of

Carnation evaporated milk and lime juice, the use of which caused my first lover, the *New York Times* bureau chief in Manila, to remark guiltily that I smelled like a puppy.

I don't test these truths every day, you understand. Augustina also warned me to beware anyone, man or woman, wearing a cape. These are just memories. Besides, whatever time it was, Cornelius was sitting on my steps. Not wearing a cape, thank God.

Lying on my steps, really, his head resting on his backpack. Legs sprawled before him, feet splayed to either side with the weight of his work boots.

From my position at the bottom of the steps, he looked dead. The night before, I had come home late to find two men urinating on the top step. When I asked if they couldn't find another place to piss, one of them, a Hispanic man, hiking his penis back into his jeans, said, how 'bout on you?

"Cornelius," I said.

He sat up in the slow, resentful way of someone who's been asleep and wants you to know it. I went up the stairs. "I hope I didn't wake you."

He did not move, forcing me to step over his legs. I took out my keys.

"I have work to do," I said over my shoulder. I could hear him pick up his backpack and get to his feet. He stood behind me on the doorstep. "I'm tired after watching Mr. Reilly have Thanksgiving," I said. "Leave your term paper with me and I'll go over it by class on Tuesday. You'll have time to fix it."

I realized that I sounded tentative, even nervous—and I was. Not because I was afraid of him, but because I did not want to offend him. I wondered suddenly if his will would be stronger than mine, if he would follow me into the building and up the stairs to my apartment and insist that I— what? read the imagined conversation with the killer John Wayne Gacy that he had written for his final paper. I have always been careful with Cornelius. I have not flirted with him. And besides, even if I had, which I hadn't, flirting is not risky. It only raises the possibility of risk.

"Was Gacy named after the actor, or is it just a family name?" I heard myself ask.

"What?" he asked.

I wondered if I was afraid of him, after all. If I really believed that Cornelius Webb was going to behave badly were I to take him and his term paper upstairs to my apartment. I had felt the palest stirring of interest when he'd pushed his leg against me in the booth, and perhaps it was that recognition that made me uneasy.

"You said you'd look at it, man." He stood close to me, both of us facing the door, our backs to the street. He was so close to me that my hip pressed against the door. "That's why I went to that place with you." He was angry.

I opened the door and we went inside. "Give me your paper," I said.

The heavy door fell closed behind us. He turned to push it with his hand, making sure that it was locked.

"I don't have it."

I stared at him.

"I threw it away."

"Why did you do that?"

"When I came from that place."

I turned away from him as if I were going to open my mailbox, and put the palm of my hand on the button that rang in my landlord's apartment. There was no sound of a bell, even though his apartment door is in the corner of the small hall, beneath the stairs. I realized that the bell did not work.

"What you need your super for? Why you vexed and all?"

I took my hand from the bell. "I want you to go," I said.

Any fragile authority I might once have had, based on my position as thirty-four-year-old teacher and his position as nineteen-year-old man, was no longer in force. Didn't mean shit in the hot and airless front hall.

I opened the interior door with my key. With one hand on the unsteady wood railing as if to pull me faster through the air, the other hand plying the opposite wall for speed, I ran up the stairs.

I was at the precinct on Tenth Street at seven-thirty that night, as I'd promised. When I said that I was there to see Detective Malloy, a large black woman at the front desk pointed upstairs.

I went to the second floor. There was a signed photograph of Gloria Estefan ("To all the kool guys in the Sixth") in the stairwell, and a reminder to sign up for Police Activity League game days, and a large placard for something called a Racket for Retiring Detectives to be held next Friday at the Castle Harbor Casino in the Bronx.

I followed the signs down a dimly lit hall to a door with a handwritten sign that said Best Homicide Squad in the World. I went inside.

A low wooden fence with a swinging gate was just inside the door. There was a row of chairs alongside the fence.

Down the center of the room was a line of gray metal desks. Swivel chairs on wheels were all around the room, the backs of the chairs draped in suit jackets. There were two desks against the back wall. There were bulletin boards covered with notices, chalkboards, boards with hooks and numbers, boards with sign-out sheets. There were old electric typewriters, a hat rack, black telephones, wastepaper baskets. There was a big clock, five minutes fast. There was a poster listing the potential offenses of sexual harassment in the workplace and a number to call should it be necessary to file a complaint. There was a red plastic bucket on one of the desks, water dripping into it from the ceiling. A narrow corridor led from the back of the room to a small cell with rusted bars.

In one corner was a room with a sign on the door reading Captain Corelli. In the other corner was a room with one glass wall. Inside the room several men in shirtsleeves were seated around a long table covered with containers of Chinese takeout, Lotto forms and a bottle of hot sauce, watching "Jeopardy!" on an old television set hung by chains from the ceiling.

I stood just outside the swinging gate. One of the men in the room with the television, a small man wearing a fluorescent green sharkskin suit, saw me and said something to a man standing in front of a microwave oven. The man at the microwave turned to look over his shoulder and I was surprised that despite the many parts of his body I would be able to identify in the dark, I had not recognized Malloy from the back.

He came out of the room, a Diet Coke in his hand. A few of the men looked at me without expression. One of them said something and the others laughed, and then they turned back to the television.

"Slow night," he said to me. "You want something to drink? A soda or something?"

He altered by an inch or two the position of the red bucket. "Leaks in the roof," he said. "They shoot down from the buildings. Twenty-two-caliber rifles."

He took me to one of the desks by the wall. On the desk was a bullwhip and a dusty plastic champagne glass and a framed black and white photograph of Buckwheat with the inscription "Thank you, Officer Malloy, You're otay." There was also a photograph of a man standing in front of a shoe repair shop.

"How you doing?" he asked. "How's everything?"

"Fine, thank you," I said, turning my bracelet on my wrist. I felt shy, and it made me uncomfortable.

"You always say that," he said.

"That's what I'm supposed to say. I could say, Yo, yo, what's up with that. But then I'd sound like an asshole. Not that people who say yo, yo are assholes. Just people who try to talk like someone else."

"Yeah," he said, smiling, looking at me as if I were nuts.

"Malloy!" someone yelled. "Your food's ready."

The man in the sharkskin suit took a tray from the microwave with a rag and held it up. It looked like a TV dinner. "Your Lean Cuisine," the man yelled.

A bald-headed man walked through the room, jacket slung over his shoulder, a small sealed urn in one hand.

"I don't care what you do," Malloy said to me, "you can do anything you want, but if you ever tell anyone I eat frozen diet dinners, I'll kill you."

I didn't say anything, trying to think who I could tell. I saw Detective Rodriguez get up from the table in the television room, stretch and yawn, and stretch again. He came into the big room and sat across from me at Malloy's desk.

"I hate 'Jeopardy!' " he said.

"Richie's favorite category is Impressionist painting. Rembrandt and shit. Right, Richie? You remember Miss—"

Before Malloy could finish, Rodriguez said, "How you doing? You doing okay?"

"I'm fine, thank you."

"That's right," Rodriguez said to Malloy. "I bet she even knows Rembrandt was the guy's first name."

"Get the fuck out of here," Malloy said. "His first name?"

Rodriguez looked through some papers on the desk. "We can close the Finklestein case. The guy confessed. I *told* you he did it, you fat fuck. Jesus, sometimes I fucking *love* being a cop." He turned to me. "I *knew* he killed his old lady when he said to me, 'You know how much I loved her? I loved her so much I used to eat her every night.' " He snapped his fingers. "*That's* when I knew."

"You have to love someone to fucking eat them?" asked a man in jeans and a windbreaker who walked past with a shotgun.

"When'd he give it up?" Malloy asked. "You put a paper bag over his head and light it, like the last time?"

"You know," Rodriguez said to him, "I was here till two in the morning last night. Finally I said, fuck you, I'm leaving. I got to be back at eight. So I leave. I come back this morning, I'm walking past the cell, he's now in the cell, and he goes, Detective, can I talk to you? I say, yeah, what the fuck do you want? He says, you really think I did it, don't you. I say, I *know* you did it. I say, not only did you do it, you probably killed the rest of your family, too. I said, you probably killed Willy, Jesus knows where *he* is. And we know you killed your old lady. I showed him pictures of her body. This is the way you left her, you asshole. This is her. This is Lillian. He said, well, I want to tell you what happened. And he broke down and gives the whole thing up. Crying and shit. It upset me, man. Usually these guys don't break down."

"It don't happen like that every time," Malloy said to me. "It's the asshole who won't talk to me that gives me a problem. Those guys are the hard guys."

"Most people think they're smarter than me," said Rodriguez. He winked at me. "And that's what gives me the edge."

Malloy walked across the room to a row of file cabinets. There was another television, a small one, attached high to the wall, with a succession of images of missing children and women and men, listing age and nickname and identifying marks, and the last place each was seen, the Wilbur G. Van Heusen Recreation Center, the Barbie Room at Macy's.

"I'm glad I got a chance to see you," Rodriguez said in a low voice.

I waited.

"I wanted to apologize. I was a little out of line the other night. In the bar. Things ain't been so good around here. Malloy might of told you."

I was silent.

"I was a little cocktailed-up." He paused. "In case you got the wrong idea."

"Wrong idea?"

"About me."

"No," I said.

"Good."

"Detective Malloy wants me to look at some pictures. He said you'd been getting them ready for me."

He frowned. He didn't seem to know what I was talking about. "Pictures?"

"Because of the other night," I said. "On West Broadway."

"Oh, pictures," he said smoothly. "No problem."

I wondered if Malloy had forgotten to tell him. For a second, I felt the hair on my arms stand on end. What my sweet Augustina used to call a cheap thrill. I looked over at Malloy, standing at an open file drawer, his back to us. He couldn't hear us.

"I thought you couldn't see his face," Rodriguez said.

"I couldn't."

"He was wearing a mask, right? So why's Malloy making you look at pictures?"

"Perhaps he was in the bar. Perhaps I'll see the face of someone who was in the bar."

"That don't mean shit."

There was a loud crack as the swinging gate was kicked open. I was the only one in the room who turned to look. An enormous, smiling, red-faced man in a pale blue suit held a young black man by the arm. He led the boy to a chair at one of the empty desks and pushed him into it. The boy wore a red bandanna around his head. When the detective let go of him, I saw the letters FTW tattooed crudely on the boy's arm.

"Hey, Richie," the detective said amiably to Rodriguez. "What's up?" He was wheezing. Perhaps because he weighed three hundred pounds.

"What's up with you, man," Rodriguez said. "I got those addresses for you, Halloran. Took me all fucking day." He said all-fuck-ing-day, breaking the four syllables equally, as if he were chanting. "You owe me big-time."

A young Hispanic detective placed five plastic containers on one of the empty desks. He opened them carefully. Black beans, rice with carrots and peas, *plátanos maduros*, pork, white flour tortillas. It made me hungry. Prepared by his mother, or his wife. A new wife, it must have been.

The young detective said to Rodriguez, "You were right about that DOA on Riverside."

Rodriguez looked in his desk drawer and carefully examined several paper clips before he found one that he liked. He began to straighten it.

"I was sure he was pushed, man," said the young detective, shaking his head. He began to eat.

"Did you look at his hands?" Rodriguez asked. "You got to look at the hands, man. You can always tell if he was pushed. If he's pushed, the natural reaction is to put your hands in front of you when you hit the ground. People that are pushed have broken fingernails. Damage to the hands. That guy was a jumper."

Detective Halloran sat on a desk. He was too big to sit in a chair. They were too far away to hear them clearly, but pieces of their conversation, if I can call it that, came across the room, especially when Detective Halloran regretfully had to raise his voice. Halloran refused to believe that the boy's last name was Kelly. "You know what that is?" he shouted at the boy. "That's a insult."

Rodriguez saw that I was listening. "Another Irish asshole," he said.

"From Ireland," Malloy said, walking by.

"You got a good memory?" Rodriguez asked me. "I mean, if I get them pictures, you'll be able to pick him out?"

"I don't think memory is very reliable. At least not my memory. My memory isn't fact."

"Yes, it is," he said coldly. "I fucking *count* on your memory."

It wasn't the time to tell him that I think memories are like dreams. Not reliable proof of anything. I can't prove a memory any more than I can prove a dream.

Malloy put a file drawer in front of me. "They're weird, those housemouses," he said. "They have their own coffee cups, you know what I'm saying?"

Rodriguez swung his legs onto the desk.

"Is Detective Rodriguez bothering you?" Malloy asked suddenly. "Telling you about the fish in the Hudson? Right under the George Washington Bridge."

"I was telling her about the time the cat ate the DOA's balls on 123rd Street."

"The time the cat ate the balls?" I asked.

"Is that so?" Malloy asked, distracted by a note that had been left on his desk.

I was not going to hear the story about the cat, I could tell.

Rodriguez took the bullwhip from Malloy's desk and stood it carefully against the wall, holding his hand in front of it until he was sure that it would not fall. "Look through the file," he said. "If he's in there, he'll jump out at you."

"I hope not," I said.

"I'd like to talk to your friend," Malloy said suddenly. "The woman who was with you."

"Pauline?"

"Yeah. Pauline."

"She wasn't there. I was alone."

"I know. I know she wasn't there. But she might of noticed someone, you know what I'm saying? Might of looked out the window."

I gave him her phone number. He took the piece of paper and went to another desk. Rodriguez was looking through a Spanish-English dictionary. I went through the index cards in the file. There were hundreds of photographs arranged alphabetically according to crime—homicide, indecent exposure, sex assaults.

A tired-looking man came out of the television room and walked to the coat stand, looking for something in the pockets of a suit jacket.

Malloy saw me watching the man. "You should know that guy," he said.

"I should?"

"That's Detective Jurowitz. He's seen more titty than any man alive."

I didn't know what to say. "Not mine," I said.

"He's in the Pussy Cat Lounge every night."

Detective Jurowitz knew that we were talking about him. "Malloy, your dinner's getting cold," he said.

"He once told me, all the peoples of the planet are linked. *Peoples*," Malloy said to me.

Jurowitz smiled. "Nice suit," he said to Malloy.

"Yeah," Malloy called back. "Always look better than them."

Jurowitz found his cigarettes and went back into the television room.

"He's supposed to have a big Johnson," Malloy said, walking to the file cabinet.

I wondered if his big Johnson was doing him much good in the Pussy Cat Lounge. I didn't think so. I turned over the cards with the desolate, terrifying faces. I didn't think that I was going to come across the image of the man who had taken me in his arms on West Broadway and Canal the other night, but I didn't want to go home.

Rodriguez was suddenly behind me. "What're you doing for dinner?" he asked quietly. "I got to get out of here."

I shouldn't have been surprised. After all, I'm supposed to like uncertainty. It interests me. The wish to be surprised, the need to be convinced.

"You like *calamar*? There's this great place on Arthur Avenue."

Malloy called out from across the room, "What I want to know, Richie, what I want to know is when you started liking white chicks."

"About the same time as you," Rodriguez said, walking away.

I was embarrassed. I looked at the picture of the man on Malloy's desk. "Is that your father?" I asked.

"Jesus," he said, coming across the room. "My father? My father was a bus driver. He's been dead fifteen years."

"I'm sorry," I said.

"It wasn't your fault," he said. "He was a gambler. A degenerate gambler. A drinker. I wouldn't say he had a drinking problem. He drank, but gambling was the problem. Horses was the problem. That's a picture of Kevin Daley," he said, looking at the photograph. "He was a great fucking detective and now he's a great fucking shoemaker. He was a detective in Narcotics when I got there in '71 and I used to make drug buys for his team. I loved working for him. He was the kind of guy who could make deductions, you know what I'm saying? He could skip from A-B-C to L and M. He had this innate ability to understand things. But he got transferred out of Narcotics. He was doing homicides. He was happy. And then late in his career, I don't know what come over him, he decides to take the sergeant's test and makes it. He's up in the Bronx. The guy no more belonged back in uniform than the man in the moon. He belonged in the Detective Bureau. So he gets to his twentieth year and his wife somehow badgers him out of the police department because she can't understand, most people can't understand, if you can retire after twenty years on half-pay, why work for half your salary by coming in every day? His whole life was the police department, but somehow she talked him into retiring. He starts teaching school in the Bronx, teaching unwed mothers and going to Iona College at night to get a master's degree. He realizes he can't handle teaching, so now he looks around and he says, what kind of thing can I do that people need? He lives in Rockland County, right around the corner from me."

"I didn't know they had corners in Rockland County," I said. Not trying to be funny. I hadn't imagined corners.

"There's corners, but there's no shoemakers. Listen to me: he comes down to the city for six months and learns the trade from an old Italian shoemaker in Wall Street, putting on heels and soles and gluing and shit. He just went and became a shoemaker. He's the best shoemaker I ever saw."

I was silent.

"When I was a kid, there was this guy named Jerry Farmer who was like a Robin Hood in the neighborhood, steal-ing bikes from the rich Jewish kids and giving them to us. He had been in prison a couple of times and he got me stealing bikes over on Fort Washington Avenue. I could've gone either way, you know what I'm saying? But there was another guy in the neighborhood, too. A young cop named Buster Kelly. I used to watch him. He had respect. He had dignity. He had a gun. He was killed trying to stop an armed robbery. There were hundreds, thousands of cops lined up at his funeral. I saw it was like this secret club. And I wanted to be in it."

Rodriguez was watching us from across the room.

I heard the boy being questioned by Detective Halloran say in an exasperated voice, "Black, spic, white, gook, it don't make no difference to us. What matters is, is you down. When we go tippin', when we set to mob somebody, you got to be with us, you got to be down, pulling the trigger, you understand?"

"You know your rights, you know that speech by heart, right?" Halloran said. "So what've you got to tell me?"

I went back to the index cards, looking at each face care-fully. Black, spic, white, gook.

"They got no place to go," Malloy said, looking at the boy. "You call them in for questioning, they actually show up. You go to bring them in, no warrant, nothing, they drop whatever they're doing, come with you. Me or you would be on the plane to Miami."

I looked up at him.

"Most people who kill, as opposed to insane killers, all they want is a reason why they did it," he said. "That's all. If you give a killer a reason, he'll take it. Does anyone really believe Robert Chambers came up with the idea of rough sex as a motive? A cop came up with that alibi. My old partner, in fact. Robert Chambers strangled that girl because she bothered him. There was no doubt in our minds that he strangled her. But he wouldn't give it up. Even *he* knew that he killed her. It was just too unbearable for him to admit. My old partner walked into the room where Chambers was being questioned and said, 'Look, Bobby, this is off the record, I'm your friend, I know what it was like, she was breaking your balls. The cunt was fucking everything that walked. She's just a stand-up blow-job. You want to go to jail for killing a fucking whore? I know what happened, Bobby: she was sitting on you, her back to you, and she was fucking you so hard your dick hurt. And she wouldn't get off you. And you reached up and yoked her off with one arm and your watch caught her in the throat, breaking that little bone there. And she died, man.' And this fucking asshole sits there a couple seconds and says, yeah, that's how it happened. Rough sex."

He pronounced whore "hoo-er."

Two detectives, one of them a woman with gray hair, came into the office through the swinging gate. The woman picked up a set of keys and made an entry on one of the clipboards. She looked at Malloy as she walked past his desk. He ignored her.

"You know," he said to me, close to me, "no normal person wants to admit that he's killed someone."

I held my finger between the faces of the two Epstein brothers, Warren and Wendell, and looked at him. He did not turn away, or speak, or swivel the chair on its rusty wheels. It was as if he were daring me to look at him, not the faces of lost and treacherous souls in the sex crimes file, and tell him what I saw.

Halloran and the boy walked through the room. Halloran had his arm around the boy's shoulder as they went through the swinging gate.

"It's too fucking busy in here," Malloy said suddenly.

Rodriguez came over. "Stop complaining. Everyone's leaving. Even I'm gone, man. I'll be in the Two-Four." He took his jacket from the back of a chair. "Maybe we'll hook up later," he said to Malloy, looking at me.

"Maybe," said Malloy. He lifted the heavy file from the desk, holding it open with one finger to save my place, and said, "Come with me."

Rodriguez smiled and left the office.

I followed Malloy into the room with Captain Corelli's name on the door, and he closed the door with his foot and put the file on a desk.

He locked the door.

I stood with my back to the desk, watching him, unsure.

He unhooked a pair of handcuffs from their resting place at the small of his back and slid them noisily across the desk.

I looked at them. I was suddenly aroused, worried that they were not for me, that he had taken them off his belt for comfort. I, who refused for years to let the husband in Paris realize his life's ambition of photographing a scorpion in my vagina.

"You're under arrest," he said.

"What did I do?"

"You don't know?"

"Shouldn't I be arresting you?"

"I don't think so," he said.

He turned me around and bent me over the desk, yanking my skirt around my waist, and pulled aside my underpants and pushed his finger, fingers, all of his fingers inside me.

"You're soaking wet," he said. He pulled my arms behind my back, holding my wrists together.

There was the sound of a belt buckle banging against the side of the desk and then the sound of a zipper. The handcuffs were on the desk, near my face.

The telephone rang in the room outside.

With one hand, he pushed against the small of my back, and with the other hand he took his penis and slid it up and down between my buttocks, wetting me, rubbing his penis with his hand, wetting it, too. And then he began to open me, first one finger, and then two, preparing me, teasing me, patient, expert, until I could feel it softening, expanding. "That's right," he said, feeling it, too. "Give it up."

"What are you doing?" I whispered. Even though I knew. It was as if I had to pretend that I did not know what he was about to do to me. Opening what was closed. Insisting. Fixing me. Unsealing me. At last. I who did not wish to belong to one man. I who did not wish to belong to anyone. I did not want to be fixed, to be held down, the closed opened, the heart broken.

I wanted to be fixed, to be held down. Opened. The old longing to be chosen, pursued, fought for, called away.

"Give it up," he said again and pushed himself into me with a sudden low moan, the force of it, the quick pain, causing me to call out. He held me tightly by the hips, moving me slowly, then faster, moving deeper, taking one hand away for a moment to wipe the base of my spine, wet with perspiration, taking my hips again, his fingers pressing into my bones, keeping me close to him. There was the sound of his breathing and another deeper, harsher sound I had not heard before as he rose slowly to orgasm, heedless of me, heedless of the men in the room outside.

He withdrew from me carefully, and turned me around. I was suddenly ashamed, ashamed that there would be an odor, or that his cock would have shit on it, and I could not look. But he held himself in his hand, wanting me to look, and I saw that there was nothing to fear.

I leaned back against the desk and reached down and found my clitoris, swollen and slippery, and while he watched, his cold blue eyes never leaving me, he talked to me in a low voice, asking me, no, telling me that I had liked it, I had liked what he did to me, I answering yes, yes, I did, until I came, fluid sliding onto the open hand he had placed under me to tilt me so he could better see it.

When I turned to go, I saw that the blotter on Captain Corelli's desk was stained.

I looked at him.

"Leave it," he said. "He thinks he's a detective. See if he can figure it out."

I've been using stand-up blow-job incorrectly. I thought it meant that the man was standing during the act, or that it was so good it deserved an ovation. But it means getting a blow-job from a girl who is short.

broccoli, n., pubic hair
everything is everything, phr., everything is cool (gang word)
down for mine, phr., able to protect oneself (as in "I be fine; I be down for mine")
hamster, n., black person (Bronx word)
to get some pink, phr., to have sexual intercourse
smoke insulation, n., smoke inhalation (misusage)

around the way, phr., in the neighborhood (as in "Tony and I be around the way tonight")

Habitrail, n., police precinct, from the plastic tubes in which small caged animals play

Phillies, n., paper for rolling a marijuana cigarette

Two, n., black person, from the code used for racial categories on police reports (One: Caucasian; Two: black; Three: Hispanic)

bloodclot, n., worst possible insult in Jamaican slang

D.T.'s, n., pl., detectives

to flake, v., to plant evidence, usually a gun

gangsters, n., pl., breasts (as in "Them two gangsters be with her all the time")

English, n., Olde English malt liquor; also O.E.

wings and things, phr., chicken and vegetables, usually Chinese takeout

Mickey D's, n., McDonald's

cocobola, n., police nightstick, after the wood from which it once was made

Things have been happening so quickly that I haven't been able to think them through. Which always makes me a little nervous. Not that anything like this has ever happened to me before. My life tends to be a little quieter than it has been for the last six weeks. I teach, I correct the work of my students and prepare my lectures, I write my own papers. I work on my book on regional slang. Sometimes I go to Easthampton on the weekend to stay with Pauline at her cottage. Usually at this time of year, when school is over, I go to see my father in Mexico City. It is not a place that I like, Mexico City. And my father does not inspire me with too much affection, either. Once when I was thirteen he left me in Geneva for five days. He later said that he had been called to Washington during a small war and it had never occurred to him that I wouldn't be all right on my own. But I know that he forgot me. Pauline says that I failed to take advantage of it, that I should have had a great time. I cannot imagine what she thinks a girl of thirteen alone in Geneva in January could have done to have herself a time. Order hundreds of boxes of chocolates sent to the room perhaps. Make a snowman. Charge a dozen linen handkerchiefs embroidered with edelweiss to her father's account.

But I am losing my train of thought (a good expression, train of thought). I need to think about murder, not fathers. Sometimes the same thing, I know, but my father was sitting in a large house in Cuernavaca with his companion, Mrs. Grummacher, drinking brandy and soda, and I was sitting on a bench in the garden of St. Luke-in-the-Fields trying to figure out if someone was trying to kill me. No metaphors here. No soul-murder. Real murder.

I bought a beer and an eggplant sandwich at Fratelli's and went to the church garden. If you walk west from Washington Square to Grove and Hudson, you will see a church of pale gray stone rising from a row of small townhouses. The banks of the river once came as far as an orchard behind the church (perhaps that is how the street was named), before Manhattan was leveled of its hills (its very name means island of the hills) and the soil pushed to the river's edge. The willows in the church garden attest to this. The trees have a look of finding themselves in the wrong place, perhaps because they remember the river moving muddily behind the apple trees. The garden is open to the public, although there are no signs to indicate this. It is a small place, hidden from view.

Sometimes there are other women in the garden sitting on the benches or on the small lawn, necking. It is a place for women who wish to be with other women. They are not self-conscious should they be surprised in the middle of a kiss, not furtive, or resentful of the intrusion. There must be a kind of downtown understanding that this is a garden in which women may come to embrace each other. Leave it to the Episcopal church to provide a haven for Lesbians.

I cannot keep to the point. Perhaps I am afraid. It is not easy for me to admit that. My courage is one of the few things about myself that I do not doubt. It is one of the things in which I believe. Passion as heroism. I have a certain earnest stalwartness, I know. A certain incautious adaptability. But I would be crazy not to be afraid now.

I keep a list in my head, on the edge of consciousness, that now and then forces me to acknowledge it: A friend, John Graham, seems to be keeping an eye on me. A student of mine, Cornelius Webb, has developed an attachment to me that may be harmless but is certainly inappropriate. He, too, seems to be watching me. Jimmy Malloy, a homicide detective, is investigating the abduction and murder of a young woman who shortly before her death was sucking his cock. Something which I now do. A rubber hand was left in the front hall of the building in which I live, under my mailbox. A man wearing black rubber and a mask followed me up West Broadway and tried to—what? rob me? kidnap me? Tried to harm me. I think that I may say that. If he had meant to rob me, he would have done so.

There. That is the list. I am by temperament drawn to

logical incompatibility, but this late concurrence of events may be too much even for me. I am always prepared, even pleased, to dispense with an expectation of causality (I was briefly a Taoist when I was sixteen and my father was in the embassy in Taiwan), but there is a danger of drifting into a certain collusive masochism. One of the things that interests me about sex is that it is a conspiracy of improvised myths. Very effective in evoking forbidden or hidden wishes. I hadn't realized I had so many of them until I met Jimmy Malloy. I still hold to the adolescent belief that one must surrender to the soul's transformation, however terrifying it may be. However difficult it may be. But I am not a masochist. I know that.

There isn't too much more they can do about the murder of Angela Sands, Malloy said when he dropped me off last night. No witnesses. No physical evidence. Only the body. Only a few parts of Angela herself. The police department does not really care that much, he said, a little bit but not that much, if different parts of a woman's body are found along the West Side Highway. They worry about the press, and they get nervous if there seems to be a pattern of killings or rapes, something that might understandably alarm the public. Most of all, he said, the police department don't want any trouble, he said. They work on the case, do what they can, but then the arms and legs of another woman, or man, or child turn up on another part of the highway and they have to move on. Sometimes, Detective Malloy said, cases are closed. Maybe forty percent of the time. But in the Sixth Precinct alone—my precinct—there are ten murders a year. One almost every month. We're only allowed to stay on a case, Malloy said, if it's someone famous. Or important. A famous dead person. Or the dead daughter of a famous person. Otherwise, we move on to the next body. A lot of what I do, he said, is border patrol, you know what I'm saying? My job is to keep bad people from good neighborhoods. I'm just riding herd.

So no one is working on that girl's murder? I asked.

It's still an open case, he said. We've had two more homicides since then. But listen, maybe there'll be a break. Rodriguez went to see your friend, by the way, and you're right, she didn't see nothing. But you never fucking know. A witness might show up. An informant. The killer might do it again and then we could start to put things together. Leave our minds open, let what we know work its way round our brain. Some smart detective might pick up something.

I'd asked him if he wanted to go to a concert with me, James Brown, and he said, maybe.

He doesn't seem to have a private life, only a secret life which appears to overlap and even be a part of his work life (the girl in the Red Turtle, the woman detective in his office, waitresses in the Bronx named Erin or Kelly). He doesn't go out to dinner with friends or women, from what I can tell, or go away for the weekend. He doesn't go to the movies. He doesn't go to baseball games. He doesn't care about restaurants. He does go to bars. With other policemen.

Like Cornelius, he is suddenly concerned about my safety. I'm not careful enough. I shouldn't take the subway. Shouldn't talk to strangers. Should lock the door. It would be easy to get into my apartment, he says, the way that I live.

Well. I don't think double-locking my door is going to keep me, or anyone else, alive. Those two girls sitting across from me on the bench, holding hands, smoking and arguing, are not going to keep their bodies intact and whole simply by locking their apartment doors at night. Their apartment door.

Maybe I should buy a dog. A German shepherd. I could move to a safer part of town. Find a nice girl myself.

I refuse to be intimidated. I will be careful, more careful than I have been. I will practice a more sustained, more attentive listening, but I am not going to change the way that I live. Because if I were really intent on being careful, I would not see Cornelius again, not out of class. I would not give him special tutoring.

I would not go to the movies with Dr. Graham.

And most important of all, I would not see Detective Malloy. I would leave him to his girls, to his wife, to the leprechauns.

You know, he said when I opened the door to get out of the car, I can remember almost every murder I ever worked on. I dream about them. It's all in my head. And sometimes something just clicks. Sometimes you got it. It's like with a broad. Sometimes you just know.

Know what? I asked.

If it's a fit, he said.

Cornelius left his term paper under my mailbox tonight when I was at the movies. I'd gone to see a documentary about the use of language by stroke victims. I don't know how he got in the front door that late at night. It is usually locked by the postman after he delivers the mail. If he delivers the mail.

Aside from a few mistakes of spelling and grammar, it is a good story.

In 1978, Mr. John Wayne Gacy was in trouble when the police dug up a dead body under his cellar. When the police were done, they had 27 dead bodies, most of them from under the house. When John ran out of room in the cellar, he buried the other bodys in the yard and some in the river.

That was 14 years ago. John has been sitting on Death Row ever since then, but he was finally put to death in May by way of a fatal injection. The ceremony was held up a couple hours when the chemicals in a tube froze up and wouldn't come thru the needle.

In those last days, I wonder if John thought about the times he used to put on his polka dot clown suit and his red nose and play with the kids. The kids liked him. He was always cool, giving them candy and shit. The clown was called Pogo the Clown and when Gacy was on Death Row, he painted pictures of Pogo the Clown which he sold. In Chicago there is a show of Pogo with one painting of an empty clown suit on a chair.

John used to work in a Col. Sanders as a manager and he said he liked all the nice folks who came in. He must of liked the food, too, cause when he ordered his final meal, he ordered fried chicken and fries. Sounds like a brother. How bad could he be?

The police say John confessed to the murders in the beginning, but you don't have to be a n***** to

know the police would. He sometimes claimed he
was innocent of the crime, and sometimes he said he
killed the first one in self-defense. Sometimes he said
he was out of town. Up to the final minute, he said
all kinds of shit. The police say the killings went
from 1972 to 1978. Six years to kill 33 people. Some
of them were raped. He must of been busy because he
was working then, organizing special parties for Pol-
ish people. Everyone says he was real popular. Maybe
that is why he could get 33 boys to come home with
him in the first place. Why he could talk them into
letting him tie a rope with a stick around their neck.

He never said he was sorry. At the end, he was
"chatty" (his guard said). He wanted to discuss the
Chicago Cubs. Eat fried chicken. Pretend he was
Pogo the Clown.

Those are the facts.

Here is the story.

It's true that as a young boy I was fascinated with
what are called animal remains. I found dead birds
on the path by the river and I kept them in shoe
boxes in my closet, making coffins for them, moving
their stiff red legs like they were dancing. But my
Dad smelled them in my room and threw them in
the fire he made in the yard to burn leaves.

I found a squirrel by the railroad track. To be honest, which is what I am trying to be in this diary, I
didn't find the squirrel. I made a trap for it and I
took it into the cellar.

I think it was a female squirrel, but it was hard to tell. I used ice cream sticks. But I could never be sure. It is easier to tell on big animals. I wanted it to be a male squirrel. I don't know why, I just did.

I was sent to camp the summer I was ten because my father said I should be out playing. At camp, you go on long hikes and row across a lake on flat rafts. It was so hot it hurt my eyes. I couldn't sleep at night. It was humid and there were mosquitoes. And tricks. You will think I mean to write ticks, but I mean Tricks. All the boys did practical jokes to each other. We did things like put slugs and frogs in peoples beds, and we did worse things. Like tie a boy to his bunk while he was asleep and then urinate on him. These things happened to me, too, I wasn't just the perpetrator. I wasn't only the bad one. I want you to know that.

In the morning after breakfast, a counselor would make you tell him if you had a bowel movement or not that day. Which I always thought was stupid, because who would say no.

I sometimes wonder during my many idle hours if it was during those many summers at the Lewis and Clark Trail Camp that I developed my love of clowns. It was there at the end of my third summer that I got to play the part of Pogo the Clown in the Camp Follys (that is what they were called).

I only wish I didn't have to wait until then to make the discovery that was to change my life. At first I didn't know how to do the clown's art of make-up and disguise, but I hope you won't think

I'm bragging if I say that over the years I came to perfect it. It is one of my real regrets that I didn't get to be a professional clown. In later years when I was day manager at the Kentucky Fried Chicken Restaurant in Ducerne, one of my steady customers, Mrs. Halle, brought me a magazine that had a place you could send away to for professional disguises and I sent away for them and that made a real difference.

But I stray from my story. I was back at Lewis and Clark making the other kids laugh. My assistant clown was Jeremy Boyd who was a very nice boy. He was good at things like back flips and cartwheels, which I'm not. I picked him as my assistant clown each summer that he was there, even though other boys wanted to do it too. Each year we got better and better. It was not true that I tried to hurt him. Even he will tell you that. I explained it then, so there is no reason whatsoever to go over old grounds now, adult men with all of our lives ahead of us.

During the time of the year when I was not at camp, and later when I grew up, I used to do my clown show at the Masonic Lodge and at ceremonies at malls and other places where the mayor or the governor would be. I went five or six times at least to the Shriner's Childrens Hospital with the Cardinal and Rossalyn Carter to entertain kids with cancer, and that was rewarding. It was those times of making those kids smile through the pain and the tears that gave me the biggest thrill of all. It was enough just to make those kids happy.

I have made nice friends here at Rock Island, too,

and I have been able to do my share to help them, too, in small ways, but I am getting ahead of myself again.

I had come a long way from playing with squirrels. So to say as they have been doing in the media that in 1969 I assaulted a eleven-year-old youth on his paper route, supposedly by inviting him into the cellar to look at my collection of stuffed birds, was and is a lie. It may be that they are confusing me with someone else. The press has to sell newspapers. I know that. We all know that. So when they said that I had invited a young man named Frances Frascotti into the cellar, some people believed it. Some people started looking at me in a different way. If they thought I was so dangerous, do they think I didn't have hundreds of chances with the youngsters who came into the restaurant all day long? or at the hospital? If I was the kind of person they think wouldn't I of had a better chance to do the things they say I did anytime I wanted? Which is more proof they are wrong.

Not that I need any proof whatsoever. I did not know that boy. I don't even SUBSCRIBE to that newspaper. I take the morning paper and I always have. Even the boy himself said when they were trying to get him into court that he *could not be one hundred per cent sure* because he was just finishing his route and it was already dark because of daylite savings time. It gets dark by the end of the afternoon. Everyone knows that. Even the boy's mother said it was a case of mistaken identity and wanted things to just return to normalcy. I was completely innocent. I wouldn't hurt those boys.

In closing, I would like to show another example of the civic sense I have always had and continue to have, ever since my happy days as Pogo the Clown and before. There is a innocent young man here named Angel Vasquez who I have befriended who is also innocent. He cannot write letters or otherwise communicate by mail with his attorney because his right hand was injured in a knife fight in the laundry. I am very glad to write his correspondence for him, as he too is a victim of the System. He dictates his letters to me and then I write them down exactly. That is his choice. I promised him I would do it. Here enclosed is a letter I wrote for him to his common-law wife Jennifer. I put it in for the record so people will know. And so he will know I did it.

Jennifer, what's up! I know already that I'll do a lot of time. I wish I was upstairs with you. I know for a fact that you better come visit me and write me every day. If you play me or if I even hear you did something, I'll fuck your ass up. If you pregnant keep it. If its a boy name him Angel Hassan Vasquez, if its a girl name it Jolin Vasquez. Send me money, about 100 or 150 and every month save 100 dollars and don't touch it. Jennifer, you know I love you infinity. Just act like nothing happen, don't think of me that much but don't ever forget me. Tell my brother I said what's up and the rest of my friends. If you have my kid tell him all good stories about me. No bad stories. Ma, I love you! Do not play me, Jennifer. And tomorrow go to the health clinic and see if you are pregnant. And get all you

*ID. Tell the cops if you can write me back. Ma, I
love you very, very, very much and I'll write your
house soon. And get a phone. Bye, but not forever.
So I see you later my secret, Ma, wife, everything.*

                                                     Angel

You love me?

I use this as an example of the kind of person I am,
someone you can see did not hurt thirty-three young
men and bury them in the cellar of my house. I wasn't
even home at the time of these alleged crimes. And even
if I was, I wouldn't do something like that. You can ask
anyone who knows me, even my ex-wife, and they will
tell you the same thing—he is innocent, he is Pogo the
Clown.

Well. Two things.

I gave Cornelius an A—how could I not?

And I want to know who really wrote that letter to
Jennifer.

Three things. I'm getting better. I don't assume that every
man with a moustache, wearing a suit, is a detective. I do
not think the new poem in the subway is meant for me. It
is a Seneca Indian song. "It's off in the distance. It came into
the room." Clearly not for me.

I went into the park this morning. There were hundreds
of people there, even at nine o'clock. Old women sat on
the benches in the shade and men were already playing chess

and checkers by the northwest corner, under the executioner's tree. A young woman was hanged from it in 1843 for murdering her employer.

The kids sitting around the dry fountain come from across the rivers, from Hoboken and Long Island City, from Staten Island and Five Towns and from the Bronx—a few of them looking to be surprised, most of them bored and edgy. The college girls, exchange students from Japan and Sweden, listen to the jumpy black boys, and the boys tie their shirts around their necks and try to give the girls a smoke or a stray dog or a good time.

There is something about the park in the summer. It is not just the smell of urine or the dust rising from the dog run and the noise of the dogs fighting, drowning out the bongo players, or the owners of the dogs screaming at the other dog owners. It is not even the dereliction, the shabbiness of the park itself, with the iron police barricades lest anyone decide to throw a few bottles. It is not the grassless enclosures full of old newspapers and cans. I will sound like Miss Burgess, I know, if I say that there is a lack of civility there. And it would be inaccurate. If anything, there is too much civility. A woman, possibly even a man, cannot sit alone on a bench for twenty seconds without being approached.

My landlord finally agreed to repair the leak in my bathroom and he arrived with the plumber, as if to punish me, at seven o'clock this morning. It turned out to be a far bigger job than he had led himself to believe, and the plumber estimated that he would be there all morning. As my landlord will not allow repairmen in the apartments unaccompanied, for fear they will steal the fixtures, he, too, was in my bathroom this morning.

So I went into the park with a banana and a container of coffee. I also took with me an article that I had noticed on Detective Malloy's desk at the station house and which I'd asked to borrow. An article entitled "The Lust Murderer," written by two gentlemen from the Behavioral Science Unit of the FBI Academy in Quantico, Virginia. There were notes on the back of it in Malloy's hand (Bullet w/out smooth oval nose like Wadcutter or hollow point makes irregular entry?—entry wound made by bullet hitting other object prior to impact—distant wound when fired beyond range of powder grains—15"–24").

I liked seeing his notes. Pauline claims that she fell in love with Leonardo Reynolds while sitting through a dress rehearsal of *Waiting for Godot* that Reynolds was directing on Broadway. Which leads me to believe that he, too, knew how the experience tends to get one's attention. I understood that I was doomed to marry Santos Thorstin when I watched him win a tennis match, 6–3, 4–6, 7–5, the summer I was eighteen. And I didn't even like him. So I was interested to read Detective Malloy's notes.

Several passages in the lust-murderer article had been underlined in ink. "Frequently the murderer will take a 'souvenir,' normally an object or article of clothing belonging to the victim, but occasionally it may be a more personal reminder of the encounter—a finger, a lock of hair, or a part of the body with sexual association. The perpetrator may also commit an anthropophagic act."

I was interested to see that the FBI thought of this as an encounter. And that the word anthropophagic had been underlined twice.

Detective Malloy still had not told me what souvenir the

killer had taken from Angela Sands. I put my coffee on the ground. I read a statement taken on September 3, 1975, by law enforcement officers in South Carolina from one James Clayton Lawson: "Then I cut her throat so she would not scream . . . at this time I wanted to cut her body so she would not look like a person and destroy her so she would not exist. I began to cut on her body. I remember cutting her breasts off. After this, all I remember is that I kept cutting on her body. I did not rape the girl. I only wanted to destroy her."

Among other things, I was thinking that it was an interesting use of the word "on," as in "cutting on her body," when someone licked my leg.

I jumped up, knocking over my coffee.

"He's happy to see you, that's all," John said, rubbing the dog between the eyes.

I sat down, hiding the article under my leg, not wanting him to see what I was reading.

"What's that you're reading?" he asked. "You looked unusually engrossed. Which is saying a lot."

"Just some research. On Gullah."

"You must be really busy," he said, sitting next to me on the bench. Skip watched me, his tongue hanging from his mouth.

"Not too," I said. "The school year is over."

"You've been going out a lot at night. I can see into the apartment from the park. When I'm on my night route."

"Your night route?"

John, who was from the Midwest, pronounced his vowels in a regional way that had once been of interest to me. Milk was pronounced melk. A golf tour was a golf terr. Route was rout.

"I've been dealing with a lot of feelings lately," he said.

One of John Graham's ways of dealing with the bad self, as he calls it, is to take his undoubtedly very justified anger and generously attribute it to someone else. He casually mentions that he has run into, oh, Jamie Saintsford, an old boyfriend of mine, at a party in Amagansett and that he, John, was made upset by it. I, slow to understand the steps of the minuet I seemed to be dancing with him, ask, why were you upset?

I really don't want to talk about it, he says. I shouldn't have mentioned it.

A few minutes will pass. The waiter comes to the table. We order. John, mindful of his health, discusses with the waiter the chef's method of preparing food. I finish my second martini, throwing it back as if I were making a wedding toast in Vladivostok.

And then he says, what upsets me if you must know is what he said about you.

About me? I ask in surprise, wondering what more Jamie Saintsford could possibly say about me, having once told the head of the classics department at NYU that I had not really ever taken to his, Jamie Saintsford's, insistence that I imitate the purring of a cat while making love.

John Graham says, Jamie thinks you really haven't written anything up to your own high standards since your article on the way Valley girls talk.

I defend myself. Worry that perhaps Jamie Saintsford is right.

Then one evening, sitting at the bar in Hermosita's, flirting with the girl bartender, tasting fifteen kinds of tequila (this bottling is a little chalkier, I remember the bartender saying around midnight), John said to me, I saw that man who teaches with you, Mr. Reilly, in the parking lot and I was disturbed by our conversation. He has some good ideas on minority college students and the different approaches to teaching them. He's not sure that you aren't making some mistakes. He wanted to go someplace and talk about you.

And I'd said, wouldn't it be easier if you just hit me once in the face, and got it over with?

What? he'd asked, shocked.

I said, I'm not sure we can be friends.

Of course, in the end it hadn't been quite as simple as that. But I didn't have to go with the bartender to a new club on West Street that didn't open until six in the morning to make my point.

A woman on the bench across from us in the park gave a man who looked as if he might be hungry a sandwich and he examined it carefully and gave it back to her.

"I was talking to my doctor about it yesterday," John said. "Talking about you, really. Well, all women, really. Women in general."

"Make up your mind."

"You. We were talking about you."

"I hope you're not going to break the rule of confidentiality and tell me what you said."

He looked confused. "*They're* not supposed to tell. I'm allowed to tell."

"No, you're not," I said.

He frowned. "I called Pauline. I hope you don't mind. I wanted to talk to you about it. Make sure you didn't kill me."

I wondered if he and his doctor had reached the part about projection yet. "Why would I mind?"

"If I didn't ask you."

"She said that you had called."

"And?"

"That's all. That you had called."

"Do you think it's a good idea? You know her better than I do. Come to think of it," he said, pausing, "I don't know you very well, either. I know you grew up in fourteen countries, that you were married to a famous photographer, that your mother drank—" He looked at me to see if he'd upset me. I was watching a young man steal a bicycle. "You had no siblings, you met your husband in Paris when you were at the Sorbonne. He was taking pictures of this old French guy who was your analyst. Or was he a Communist? I can't remember." He looked at me again. "So far so good?"

"Not really." Not a good word, sibling.

I sometimes think that he has all his information, all his means of reference, from gossip columns and television. Like Rodriguez, he seems to think that memory is fact.

"I've been having these funny panic attacks lately," he said. "At least, I *think* they're panic attacks. They're pretty bad."

I felt sorry for him. The fact that he sees himself as an organism, a valuable and unique organism, which of course he is, in fascinating flux, worthy of constant study, does not mean that he doesn't suffer.

"What happens?" I remembered that last spring he had lost his hearing for eighteen hours.

"Sweats. I don't know where I am. My mind races. I feel like if I started to run, I'd never stop."

"I'm sorry," I said. He held out his hand and I took it.

"I think it may have something to do with something I

heard when I was a kid. Something I *think* I heard. Actually, I know, know for a fact, that I heard something."

I let go of his hand.

"Hasn't that ever happened to you?" he asked. "You get these funny images like you saw or knew something? Weird memories from childhood."

The dog leaned over and licked my shoes.

"My childhood is like a dream," I said. "I'm not sure it's possible to look at it with too much expectation of meaning. I'm not even sure you're supposed to. Expect too much from memory."

"And you don't mind?"

"No. In some ways it is a relief not to have to understand everything."

He was silent. "I just wish I didn't have these funny attacks," he said fretfully. "My brain, my brain practically explodes. I've been thinking of going on that medicine."

"Yes," I said. "Perhaps you should." He began to rub his ears and I said, "You have good reason to be unnerved. Your medical boards next month. Not much money. Starting a practice later than most. A sick father. Is your father still sick?"

He nodded.

"It will be two hundred degrees in the subway in an hour. And there's Bellevue itself."

He looked at me. "I feel so much better."

"When are you seeing Pauline?"

"Oh, she'll eat me alive. Are you kidding? She's worse than you."

"I'm seeing her Friday night," I said. "Maybe we'll eat

each other alive." Funny, I thought. I'd just been reading about anthropophagy.

"Well," he said, getting up, "I see that Skip has washed your feet like the wine and the fishes."

I knew better than to ask what he meant. It wasn't even a mixed metaphor. A mixed parable.

"Frannie, did I ever tell you my mother dressed me in girls' blouses until I was seven?" Skip had leapt to his feet in his eagerness to go, but on hearing John's tone of voice, he sat down again.

"You did," I said, lying.

"Perhaps this is why I have this fascination with Pauline. The way that she dresses. The other night she was wearing a dress made entirely of those little rings—you know, the kind on soda cans." He stared at Skip for a moment, think-ing. "I walk by your apartment often. Sometimes that car's parked in front, so I don't ring the bell."

"Car?" I was surprised.

"What are you doing tonight?" he asked.

"I'm seeing *Eugene Onegin*." I always wonder if seeing is the correct verb to use in regard to an opera. Although hear-ing *Eugene Onegin* would not be altogether right, either. I would not normally tell him what I was doing. Something about him made me uneasy. "It is that very beautiful produc-tion that was done last summer at Glyndebourne. It is full of shocking, shocking for opera, meant-to-be-unconscious ges-tures. After the letter scene, Tatiana pours a ewer of water over her head. I think you'd like it."

"*You* like it. I probably wouldn't. I'm really only interested in my own behavior."

Skip, hearing something new in John's voice, began to

strain at the leash. They went off, John stopping once to retie his laces. Leaving me with lust murder and an empty cup of coffee.

He called me Wednesday night on his way to a murder, a good murder as opposed to a bad murder, he said, which meant a real person, not a drug dealer. When a drug dealer is killed, it is called a C.C.—Condition Corrected.

"I just wanted to let you know I'll be out of town a couple of days. You won't be able to reach me. I'll be back on Friday in time for my four o'clock tour."

"Where are you going?" I asked, wincing, breaking all of my rules. I put my hand over my eyes. The charms on my bracelet felt cool against my face.

"To the shore. It'll be nice. I need a break. Give me some time with my kids. You never see your kids if you're a cop."

"How old are your kids?"

"Eighteen and twenty."

"Eighteen and twenty?" I was surprised.

There was something different in his voice, as if he were hurrying me along, moving me past something before I saw it.

"Your wife going, too?"

"Yeah," he said quickly. "My ex-wife."

"No," I said. "Your wife."

"Get the fuck out of here! I sleep on the fucking sofa."

"You may sleep on the sofa," I said, "but she's your wife."

There was a long pause. He was deciding. "Listen," he finally said, his voice low, "I can't really talk here, you know what I'm saying? I'm at a disadvantage here. I'm in my of-

fice, there's people all the fuck over the place. There was a
contract killing in the Thirteenth, there's fucking cops
everywhere. You know what I'm saying?"

"I didn't think I seemed like the sort of person who would
mind."

"What?"

"I'd have fucked you anyway."

There was another pause. I could hear voices in the background. "I thought I'd lose you," he said at last.

"Have you ever told me the truth?"

"Look—" He paused. "People lie to me all day long. And
I lie to them all day long. I've done it all my life."

He was always a few steps ahead of me. He was on Jupiter
while I hurried across Nineteenth Street. He was convincing.
Lying as cultural attribute. A hazard of the job. And I fell
for it. It did not occur to me then that he lies simply because
he likes it. Lies to bosses. Lies on the stand. He boasts about
it. Lies under oath. It's called testilying, he'd told me. Lies
to women, especially to women. Starting with his mother
and working his way through all of us. His wife. The doll
collection. He couldn't be bothered to tell the truth.

"You haven't lost me," I said quietly.

"I feel sick about it. Like I've fucked everything up."

"How long will you be at the shore?" I asked. Jealous.

"It's been planned all year. I can't get out of it. I would if
I could. We got the house with my cousin, really it's her
cousin, but I call him my cousin. It's all paid for."

I was silent, my mind racing.

"I probably won't be able to call you."

"No. Probably not."

"You know, Sergeant Engelhardt used to say, you're going

to end up the most fucked-up individuals on the face of the earth. Your wives will hate you, half of you will be alcoholics, the other half will be just plain nuts. You won't have a friend who's not a cop, and you will hate everyone else. You think you're going to kick the shit out of the world, but the world is going to kick the shit out of you." He paused. "You know, it's not a particularly hard job. There's right things and wrong things. It's simple. You don't have to be that smart to be a cop."

His self-pity made me dislike him for the first time.

"What're you doing? You writing?" he asked.

"Yes. Always. I'm seeing Pauline on Friday. After the concert." I was finding it difficult to speak with any vivacity, any pleasure. I wanted to get off the phone. I wanted him to feel bad, too. "It's that concert you couldn't go to," I said.

"Oh, yeah," he said.

"I'm going with someone I met at a party." Lying.

"Good," he said. "That's good. Listen, I'm sorry I couldn't make it." Lying.

"Yes. Well."

It was very noisy at his end of the phone. Maybe he really was at work. "I have to run," he said. "They're yelling at me. They can always tell when you're talking to a broad." He laughed at something someone said to him. "I'll call you when I get back," he said.

I'm not going to the James Brown concert. It is not the sort of thing you go to alone. I can go alone to hear the Bach cello sonatas, but not the Godfather of Soul. I gave the tickets to

Cornelius, who is taking his sister. His sister named Jennifer. Who gets letters from her boyfriend in prison. She *is* pregnant, it turns out. I told him I would do what I could to help her. He was happy with the tickets, and happy with his A. He asked if I would be able to see him on the weekend. He has something he wants to show me.

Pauline was having drinks at the Carlyle with her new eye doctor, Dr. Whyte. An odd configuration, I thought, but not unethical, as she quickly assured me. Not that I'd thought it was. Or cared. Dr. Whyte was married, she assumed, and had a limp. She said their flirtation had begun during a recent checkup while she was sitting in that special chair, her head in a metal clamp to better facilitate the examination, to better facilitate their knees touching in the dark.

I was meeting her at eleven at the Pussy Cat Lounge. I had not spoken to her for a few days. Perhaps because I'd turned off the phone. I didn't stray too far from home (not leaving the house), eating bowls of cereal (sometimes without milk), listening to opera (*Madama Butterfly*, two thousand times). Brushing my teeth, taking a bath, of course, changing my nightgown, but not really combing my hair. So it was a good thing that Pauline, after leaving several messages on the machine ("The trouble is, I mean what worries me, worries me a lot, is that he doesn't understand you, he doesn't *get* you. He doesn't know you really are the sexy girl with glasses"), thought it would cheer me up to take me to the Pussy Cat.

I dressed and decided to walk to Church Street. It would

be good for me. A little air. A little exercise. A little downtown. I brushed my hair.

If I'd only known.

Pauline was not in the Pussy Cat Lounge. I ordered the tequila that she likes, eager to hear about her rendezvous with
Dr. Whyte. She told me on the phone that he'd admitted that
her vision was perfect, adding the rather inaccurate remark
that love was not blind. I said it sounded like a line he might
have used quite a few times. Oh, God, I hope so, she said.

At eleven-forty, I put on my glasses and began to watch
the hockey game on television. I ordered a cheeseburger and
asked Tabu to check with the bartender to see if Pauline had
telephoned.

There were two men at the next table. When they realized
that I was eating alone, one of them, a man with a moustache
and a tattoo on his shoulder of a leprechaun in a top hat, slid
into the chair next to me.

"How you doing?" he asked.

"Fine," I said. "Thank you." Always a lady.

"What's up?"

"A friend of mine, my boyfriend actually, says that every
Irish guy he ever locked up has that tattoo."

He laughed.

I got up from the table, leaving my cheeseburger behind.

"What'd I say?" he asked his friend.

The Vietnamese gentleman who owns the Pussy Cat
Lounge happens to be the owner of the building. I knew that
a set of keys to the two apartments upstairs was kept behind
the bar because Pauline had had to borrow it many times. I

asked the bartender for the keys. I wanted to wait for her upstairs.

"Alone," I said to make the bartender smile.

"Whatever, babe," she said.

I do not remember too much now. Certain things. Certain images. All sorts of irrational, irrational because nonsensically inappropriate, pieces of information stream through my head, as if my unconscious were bombarding me with words and phrases, an enemy agent subverting a radio broadcast. The sentence "General Ameglio, an Egyptian, could dance the polka with a pack mule across his shoulders" is still going through my head.

Detective Malloy was there, I know. Not at first. Later. I don't know exactly when he was there, soon, rather early on, before the others.

Detective Rodriguez told me Malloy was there. That at least is what he says. That Malloy came right away. I thought he was with his wife.

I do believe that it was Malloy who cleaned me up. The blood. It is a commonplace, I know, about blood. You don't realize how much blood is in one person's body. There was vomit, too, and because I could not remember, they had to do tests to see whose vomit it was.

They had very experienced crime-scene detectives there, Malloy says. A friend of his named Detective Sherman who is famous for his ability to ascertain precisely whether a fistful of rice taken from the stomach of the deceased is white American rice or spic rice or Chinese rice. That is what Malloy said.

Sometimes when I am not expecting it, when I let down my guard for a moment, allowing the thousands, the millions of little synapses in my head to work their will, conveying to me just what it is that I cannot bear to know, cannot bear to be known, I do remember.

Malloy was there.

He did clean me up.

It was my vomit. I could have told them that. If I'd remembered.

It was Malloy who took her head, lifting it from the sink where I'd put it for safekeeping. Where I could watch it and keep it safe.

Malloy asked me to come downtown again today to look at more photographs. He was waiting for me. We sat at a table inside a big room. Clerks and police assistants, most of them women in jeans and sweatshirts, worked at computers or leaned against the open drawers of file cabinets using both hands to whisk through the files.

"I was at the morgue," he said as he sat down across from me. "That's why I couldn't pick you up."

"I don't want you to pick me up."

"No problem," he said calmly.

"Why were you at the morgue?"

"I'm a policeman."

"Oh. That's right. I forgot. I thought you were one of those married guys who believe there's no such thing as a bad blow-job."

"You know," he said, "some women are terrible blow-jobs. No rhythm. No sense of cock."

He turned a quarter with his fingers, as if he were practicing a magic trick. As always, I was pulled in by the small gesture. It was all that I knew about him, and it was perilous to me. "No sense of cock. Good phrase. Yes, that must be terrible."

I was suddenly tired, as if I hadn't the strength, or the interest, to fight him. "Why were you at Pauline's?"

"I just told you. I'm a policeman." He paused. "I was walking in the station-house door when they got the call."

"Who called?"

"The girl downstairs. The bartender."

I looked at his hands again, and made myself look away. I closed the heavy book of photographs that he had opened in front of me and pushed it to the center of the desk.

"Listen," he said, "I'm *always* going someplace where someone is dead, only this time it was your best friend. These kids, the young uniform guys, said we got a female and someone tried to take her head off. I'm always expecting the worst, even after all these years. Your imagination makes it worse and then you see it and you say to yourself, it's not so bad as I thought. The body is never in full view. Never. I have to find it. I'm in a strange room, I'm looking for it, then boom! there it is. I'm always worried that I'll see something that will make me sick, something that will make me run away. That there will be one body and I'll say, that's enough, and walk away. But what happens is you see the body and something in you takes over—how was she cut? where? who is she? You're either a good detective or you're not. You either get down on your knees and put your nose in the wounds, or you don't. My tie sometimes gets bloody when I bend over. I forget to tuck it into my shirt."

I looked at his tie and he ran it between his fingers, starting at the knot. There was no blood on it.

"Will you tell me?" I asked.

"Tell you what?" He spoke flatly, as if he dreaded my question and already knew that he would answer it.

"What you did."

"Why do you think that knowing makes a difference?"

"I've thought that all my life."

"Well, you're wrong. Knowing don't mean shit."

"Doesn't mean shit."

He took a breath. "You black out everything else in your mind and you become logical. You begin to put it together. Slowly. You take a flashlight and you go over every inch of the body. You look at scars, tattoos, wounds, fingernails, ears. You look to see if her pants have been pulled open, if there are semen stains, if she has her period. Your whole world at that moment comes down to that body."

"Like sex."

"No. Not like sex." He refused to be provoked. "Killing is a very personal thing. Not like sex at all. It's only the methodical killer who makes it a personal act. It's not some drug dealer in Harlem blowing a hole in someone's head because he happens to be on his block. This was premeditated. He watched her. He watched your friend. He followed her on the street. He knew her routine. Maybe he even spoke to her, spoke to the two of you, got into the same elevator, asked for directions in the subway. Maybe he bought her a drink in a bar and told the bartender not to tell her it was from him. Your friend gets her tequila and looks up and six different guys are staring at her down the bar."

"That's not what I meant."

"What?"

"I want to know what you did with her."

He looked at me. "Why?" he asked at last.

"I don't know. So I can imagine it. So I can sleep."

He started to speak, then stopped himself. Then he began again. "She must have been moving," he said quietly. "He slashed at her neck, and across her breasts. Her throat was cut through the windwipe. The jugular. The epiglottis. The tongue. He held her by the hair and he cut all the way around and he moved the head back and forth. When you get to bone, you have to find your way between the vertebrae. You need a bigger knife. He had a bigger knife. It's not easy to put a knife through bone. It's hard. But he did it." He paused. "And I can tell you something else. He liked it."

"Yes," I said. I didn't want him to stop.

"He pulled the drain in the shower before he left. Took out anything that could help us. It bothers me. He knew about drains."

He handed me his handkerchief and I wiped my face and thought how generous it was of him to spoil his look by taking it out of his pocket. He was very conscious of the way that he looked.

I am so ashamed by the things that used to make me unhappy. That I was upset because he lied to me about his wife and then went on vacation with her. That Yale University won't give me permission to use the letters of C. K. Whitney. That my father forgot me in Geneva.

"Do you know how close you came to being killed?" he said quietly. "You were at the front door as he went out the window. He left a duffel bag on the fire escape. Rubber-lined, waterproof. And he left a print that don't match up with regular shoes or sneakers. He's good." He sighed. "I took the duffel bag to the morgue. The M.E. and I tried to put her together on the autopsy table. The wounds on her body were consistent with those on the body of Angela Sands."

I wiped my face again.

"Is that what you wanted? You satisfied?"

I nodded.

"A killer will leave certain identifying traits behind whether he wants to or not," he said in a low voice. "Does he cut the neck in the same place? does he shit on the floor? urinate on the body? jerk off on the body? leave it in a suggestive pose? He may even have a sense of humor. But whatever he does, it will always be the same. And that's what tells me. That's how I know. You don't look for the discrepancies, you look for the similarities.

"What is the *same* about this crime scene?" he went on, running his hand through his hair. "Maybe he slips the lock, maybe he cuts from left to right, maybe he attacks from the rear. Maybe he strangles her first. Maybe he makes a sandwich before he leaves." He pushed his chair back from the desk. "There were smear patterns of blood around the apartment," he said. "Which means that he played with the body."

I felt as if I couldn't breathe. "If I had gone upstairs sooner."

"You didn't do nothing wrong." He waited until I got my breath. "Are you all right? I'm worried about you." He stood and came around to my chair.

I didn't want him to touch me. And he didn't.

"I'll take you home," he said. "I'm going back to her apartment. There's something I know but I don't know it yet. It's driving me nuts. Sometimes it helps just sitting at the scene."

"How will you get in?"

He looked surprised. "I have a key."

"A key? Her key?"

"I guess so. I have *a* key."

I got up and walked to the door. "You were there so soon," I said. "I thought you were at the shore with your wife."

He had his hand on the doorknob, but he let his hand fall to his side.

"You're not trying to kill me, are you?"

"Get out of here," he said, and pulled open the door and I walked out.

I went to play tic-tac-toe with the chicken in the Chinese video arcade. The videos aren't Chinese, just the boys who play them.

I was thinking about regret, walking down Centre Street. Most people insist that they don't have regrets. Which I think is a mistake. I think that regrets are important. I like them. Or rather, I like my own. The only trouble is that regrets, especially those of other people, tend to be sentimental, as in "I regret that I was sick the weekend of Woodstock," or, the most sentimental of all, "Je ne regrette rien." To prove my point, I admit that I was regretting that I had never taken Pauline to play the chicken. She would have been especially pleased if the animal rights' activists had been picketing outside. She used to say that you could sit in a silent movie theater and watch children being tortured to death, but the moment an armadillo appeared with a thorn in its paw, people began to sob.

I knew that I could play to draw. But that is only because I've practiced. Cornelius told me the chicken comes from a research center in Arkansas called the IQ Zoo, not far from where the President lived as a child. The IQ Zoo trains animals to perform tricks. When I asked Cornelius what tricks exactly, he said, well, they have a Wild West show where bunnies shoot it out with tiny guns and holsters and shit. It was Cornelius who first took me to see the chicken. After I lost, I went home and drew small grids on a piece of paper and made the chicken's first move. The chicken always gets to go first. And it always puts an X in the top left square. That is how it beats you. Unless, of course, you know to put your mark immediately in the center square. Then you tie. Cornelius says that it isn't fair that the chicken is allowed to go first. The chicken is better, he says, because it gets to play all the time. I didn't tell Cornelius that I had figured out how to tie the chicken by working out on paper every possible move.

I thought if I played tic-tac-toe with the chicken on Mott Street with the Asian (not Oriental, Cornelius says) boys playing Mortal Kombat all around me, I might receive some sign that would make me feel better. It was not that I was looking for some explanation of man's inhumanity to man. I was past that. I was just looking for a little wit.

When I asked the vendor, an Armenian man with no love of Asians, or chickens for that matter, why the chicken's glass box was empty, he shook his head and said that the chicken was out. He was watching CNN on a tiny television.

It began to rain in that rushed and urgent way that it rains in New York. The rain sounded very loud on the aluminum awning of the arcade. Two women stood under the awning holding newspapers over their heads. One of the women said something to me and I looked at her and there was a photograph of Pauline in her Marilyn Monroe white pleated dress, a little damp, over her left eye. It was the picture Pauline's mother in Belfast had given the press, and I thought it was a very good choice. Pauline had always spoken sweetly of her mother. She had made clothes for Pauline when Pauline was a girl, copying the dresses from photographs of movie stars that Pauline kept in a scrapbook.

I stepped out into the rain and walked to the subway station at Chambers Street. A woman on the platform dropped a gum wrapper to the ground, and when I pointed out that littering was a public offense I realized that I might be looking for trouble of a kind that might once and for all satisfy me. Her two girlfriends looked at me as if I were crazy. By the time the woman told me to go fuck myself, I was at the far end of the platform, thinking about Malloy. Imagining that he was waiting for me. That I would get home and he would be in front of my building. That he was worried about me. That he was following me.

I looked over my shoulder. He was not there. Only a small jazz combo trying to sound like Sonny Rollins. A man who looked like he might know how Sonny Rollins was supposed to sound waited for the train with his hands over his ears.

There was heat lightning on the way home. The trees in the park swayed and shuddered in anticipation, with delight or dread I do not know. I stopped at the Strand and bought a book. Taber's Cyclopedic Medical Dictionary.

I made myself two martinis and got into bed in my clothes and looked up epiglottis. Pauline would have been pleased. Not that I was in bed wearing a dress, but at the definition of the word. "A thin leaf-shaped structure . . ." She would have liked the "thin" even in regard to the covering of her larynx. The covering that prevents liquids from entering the airways. The airways. Liquids like maple syrup. Diet Coke. Semen. A girl was grateful to the epiglottis for keeping her airways clear.

Hyoid bone. That delicate bone "shaped like a horseshoe." A lucky horseshoe hanging at the base of her throat.

Carotid, internal. From the Greek, *karos*. Deep sleep.

Cerebral, communicating. That sounded like bad poetry. But then I found "semi-lunar." I would like to think that her carotid artery was a half-moon, helping that cautious duenna of an epiglottis.

I looked up all sorts of things (lymph, for example, and Significance of Change in Urine—should urine have a slightly spicy odor, it is an indication that sandalwood has been ingested), and by the time that I got to carphologia (the involuntary plucking of bedclothes), I was a little drunk.

When I tired of holding the heavy book on my chest, I wondered who I could call on the telephone. I couldn't think of anyone except Malloy. I wanted to talk to him. To hear his dangerous voice, the voice that he used with women ("Hi, baby, how you doin'? Sittin' on the phone?" The "hi" drawn out in a low, implicating whisper). I wanted to hear the coldness that was so deep it went beyond the man-bitch thang, as Cornelius would say. That coldness of spirit that had made it so thrilling to get his attention.

I know the sort of man who likes me. So I wondered, not for the first time, what secret I might possess, what magic charm or talisman had allowed me to get Malloy's attention in the first place. To get him to fuck me. I am not the kind of woman he likes. I'm not a nurse. I'm not going out with any of his friends. I'm not married. I'm not a stewardess. I'm not blond. Perhaps he thinks I'm rich. I don't even know if it's about sex. He doesn't talk about sex the way some men do, wanting to go over it, wanting to hear the woman describe what it was like, how she hadn't been able to wipe herself for a week. He did ask me one thing—if anyone had ever fucked me the way he had in the captain's office, and I said yes. Lying.

When I was fourteen and having a little trouble holding the attention of the son of the German ambassador to the Philippines, a mute boy (metaphorically mute) named Gunter, Augustina had said harshly, put yourself in his way, girl. If he's coming down the boulevard, you got to lay there on the pavement in front of him so he is forced to step on you, so he will say, what are you doing there, girl?

What *am* I doing there? I'd asked her. I still don't know.

There was the sound of the doorbell.

Malloy. Malloy arriving just in time. I jumped up, thinking that at least I was dressed, it had been a good idea after all to get into bed fully clothed.

I ran down the stairs, a little unsteady, a little dizzy, my heart leaping in triumph, and I opened the door and there was Cornelius.

"I heard about your friend," he said. He was wet. Drops of rainwater glistened on his dreads.

"Yes," I said. Disappointed. "Women are wearing her on their heads."

"I saw it on television," he said.

Oh, I thought, if it was on television, it must be true.

"She was wearing a dress made of tinfoil and shit."

"One of her favorites. I don't remember the shit."

"I'm writing a screenplay," he said.

"About Pauline?" I was shocked.

"No, man, about John Wayne."

"Oh," I said, nodding, relieved. "The actor?"

He shook his head. "My man. My man Gacy."

I didn't know what to say.

"You been working on that word book?"

"No," I said. "I can't work. It embarrasses me."

I opened the door wider, letting him inside the front hall. He looked down at my feet.

"Why you wearing only one shoe?"

I gestured behind me. When I run downstairs without the key to open the front door, I put one shoe in the interior door to keep it from closing behind me.

Cornelius nodded. I could tell that he wanted to come upstairs. But Malloy was coming. It was only a question of time. I didn't want Cornelius to be there when he arrived.

"Come in," I heard myself say.

I went up the stairs, Cornelius behind me. There was the sound of rain on the skylight at the top of the stairwell. I could faintly hear the song playing on his Walkman. I wondered if he was listening to Smif 'n' Wessun. If he was looking at my ass as I walked ahead of him, trying to hold my body still, trying not to move in any way that might be thought an invitation.

He put his hand on my leg.

I stopped, my leg extended behind me, his fingers sliding down my calf to the ankle. For the briefest moment, so fast that it was nearly an unconscious thought, not unconscious enough, I imagined him hurting me. Holding me down on the stairs.

I turned to face him, my foot in his hand, and sat on the stair above him. I took his head in my hands. He was still wearing his earphones, and my hands held them to his head.

He smiled. My skirt was open. My foot resting in his hand. I was thinking that everything had changed in an instant, changed in a way that neither he nor I might mind, when he leaned over and pulled something from my leg.

"You got a leaf on you," he said.

My foot fell from his hand.

I stood up, flushed, no longer worried about my ass. I went up the stairs.

He followed me into the apartment, dropping his backpack onto the sofa. "My sister said to thank you," he said.

I went into the kitchen. "Your sister's boyfriend Angel killed someone," I said. "John Wayne Gacy left that part out."

"It's because you and me don't never talk. It's always just jive." He came into the kitchen behind me. "We're always warring," he said.

I hesitated. "I don't know how else to make it equal between us."

He looked at me. "What kind of shit is that?"

"I don't mean color. Or race. I mean something else."

"What?"

"If I can use language in a way that is ironic, and playful, it makes it easier."

He was looking at me in a way that he never had before. Impatient. A little bored. As if I were not so smart after all. "What is it you trying to say?"

"That you shouldn't be here."

"Why not?"

I lost my nerve. "I'm expecting someone."

"Fuck that, man."

"Fuck what?"

"That, man."

I was silent.

"You got something I could drink?"

"What do you want?"

"I'll take a soda," he said quietly.

His sudden falling-away, his tentativeness, his loss of will, made me dislike him, and I realized that I was disappointed.

I opened a Coke for him. The window was open and I could smell the rain and the wet dirt from the dog run in the park. There was a man standing in the bushes behind the iron fence railing, looking up at the window.

I could see Cornelius's reflection in the raised window-pane, against the sycamore trees. It would soon be night. Dark along the island. I thought of the rivers that coursed the island and I wondered if sycamore was an Indian word, the idea of the river making me think of Indians. There was a stream that once ran through Washington Square Park, a *kuyl* as the Dutch called it, a wide stream running south to the tip of Manhattan, flooding into marshes full of wading birds and wild fowl. The Minetta. An Indian word. It is a sentimental idea, I know, thinking about Indians and fresh-water streams flowing under Sixth Avenue. Cornelius looks a little like an Indian, with his dark skin and his handsome beaked nose.

Which was two inches from the back of my neck. Nape of my neck. Nape is a word that makes me think of Japanese women, women of the Heian period, the nape being that pale band between the padded collars of seventeen silk gauze kimonos and the black line of lacquered hair. Also, to be fair, nape brings to mind the neck—rosy, flushed, damp—of certain half-clothed French women in eighteenth-century paintings. Boucher. Powder from the woman's hair-dressing sifted onto a bare plump shoulder as the gentleman tries to prevent her from leaving the room. A little like Cornelius.

Cornelius was brazen.

Brazen is a good word.

I was brazen.

I turned and kissed him, pulling his head toward me, cupping his ears like shells, my Scallop shells of quiet. Nowhere could I find peace.

He pulled away from me stiffly—not loose, not fluid, the joints hinged not for mobility, but for some other thing—and took the hem of my dress and pulled it over my head, waggling my arms, yanking the collar when it caught in my hair.

He unfastened my brassiere, releasing the clasp between my breasts, no lesson needed from the Chicken Lady. He stepped away, and looked at me.

My back was to the window. The man in the park was watching me, too. I was between them.

He unbuttoned his jeans and reached inside and lifted his penis, raising one leg to find it, laying it in the fork of the seam. He was not circumcised and it looked the way all uncircumcised penises look to me—like the snake in the Garden of Eden. I was thinking about that, my heart suddenly full of despair.

I'd kissed him on the mouth, put my tongue in his mouth, and I knew that I did not know how to stop it. I had forgotten how to stop it. Because it is something that women know how to do. Oh, I don't mean how to stop Cornelius, I mean how to stop myself.

He moved his hands across my breasts, pinching my nipples, putting his mouth on my nipples, licking them, sucking them. I could feel the quickening between my legs, the contracting of muscle, the belligerent glad rush of blood.

I pushed him away.

He looked at me. Veiled. Heavy-lidded. Displeased.

"I don't want to do this," I said.

He stepped back. He had an erection. "You don't like it?" He rubbed himself with one hand. "My dick's so sweet, it'll give you cavities."

"Yes, I like it. But I don't want you to do it." I bent over to pick up my dress and he put his hand on the back of my head. Holding me down.

"I didn't want to fuck you anyways," I heard him say.

I was silent. Listening. Afraid, now that I knew what I wanted. What I did not want. I did not want him to hurt me.

"What you want me to do?" he said, whispering in my ear.

I was silent.

"What?" he asked.

"Let me go."

"What, girl?"

"Cornelius."

"I knew you'd fuck me up," he said. His hand loosened its grip, then dropped away. He went into the living room and picked up his backpack.

"What you going to do?" he shouted back at me.

I stood in the kitchen door, holding my arms across my breasts.

"Do?"

"You know," he said.

"I don't."

"You going to fuck me up?"

"Why would I fuck you up?"

"You be looking to fuck with me since day one."

There was a sound at the window, as if a small bird had flown into the glass. I turned. There was nothing. I turned back to Cornelius.

He was putting something into his backpack. "You done fucking with me?"

"Yes," I said. I put on my dress. "I wasn't fucking with you."

There was another sharp crack at the pane. I went to the window. Detective Rodriguez was in the street, standing next to a gray car. He waved at me. I looked back at Cornelius, but he was not there. The door was open.

I ran down the stairs. I opened the street door and stood at the top of the stoop. The rain had stopped.

"Malloy asked me to make sure you were home," Rodriguez called up to me. "If I was in the neighborhood. See if you was all right."

I nodded.

"Well?" he called.

"Well what?"

"You all right?"

"Why wouldn't I be?"

He smiled.

"Where is he?" I hadn't meant to ask. My head ached.

He shrugged and opened his hands as if to ask, how would I know?

"Tell him not to bother me."

He laughed. He got into the gray car and I waited until he pulled away. I went inside.

I picked up the can of Coke that Cornelius had left on my desk. I put it in the sink. I turned off the kitchen light. I went into the living room, my brassiere in my hand, and remembered the man in the park. I turned on the CD player, Al Green, and went back to the window to see if the man was still there. Wondering if he, too, had lost interest. He had.

I turned off the light on my desk. My mother's jade hairpins were gone.

"I'd like to report a theft," I said.

"You have the wrong office. I'll transfer you to Robbery."

"What about rape? You do that?"

"That would be Sex Crimes."

"What about attempted murder?"

"That's closer. Better if you're dead."

I didn't say anything.

"Did you hear me?"

"Twenty-one Washington Square."

"Is that the location of the body?"

I hung up.

"You look all right to me," he said, brushing past me. "You still pissed?" He went into the kitchen and took off his jacket and poured some bourbon into a glass.

"I like Al Green," he said. "When I was an undercover, I used to go to see him at the Copa. Look," he said, putting down the drink on an article about preliterate tongues in Japanese aboriginals, "we got a problem here."

I moved aside the papers. "Do we?" Literate tongues.

"Listen, you don't want me. Only you don't know it. You just think you do. I've been thrown out of a lot of places."

"That sounds like a boast."

"What the fuck do you want from me?"

I looked at him, the offense I felt making me blush.

"I don't know if I can be who you want," he said. "You know what I'm saying? A broad wants me to be one way, wants something from me, I can do it, I told you that already, but with you, it's different. I feel like I'm running all the time. Running just to stay even."

"I'm sorry." I was furious.

"You didn't do nothing."

"I know. I'm sorry that you feel that way."

He nodded. Softening. "You're not easy."

"Why would you want me to be?"

He shrugged. "You know what's wrong with you? You know your worth. You know just how much you're worth."

"That's why I'm not easy?"

He thought for a moment. "Yeah." He paused, as if I really wanted him to come up with the right word. "Yeah. Exhausting. You know, sometimes things are just what they are. Nothing more. You're smarter than I am. But sometimes things are simple. You're always looking for something more. Beneath, above, down the fucking sides. And sometimes you get it wrong."

"I'm sure I do."

He looked puzzled. "So why don't you stop? Stop analyzing every fucking thing." He pronounced the word "every" as if it had three syllables.

"I thought you liked it," I said.

"I did. At first."

I waited for him to go on.

"You know, I was doing just fine before I met you. You know that? Just fine."

"Hustling blow-jobs in the Bronx."

He took a drink. "What's wrong with the Bronx?"

"It depends on what you want," I said, walking behind him. "Maybe you don't know what you want."

He ran his hand through his hair. "Maybe I don't."

I went to him. I put my hand on him. Sometimes it's hard to tell whether you've got the balls or the penis, but I had no trouble with him. He started to get hard the minute I touched him. Maybe he was already hard.

"What do you want from me?" he asked again.

"You'll see."

He paused. "Will I like it?"

"I think so."

"You're not sure?"

"No, you're not sure."

I lifted his handcuffs from his waistband. He reached behind instinctively, but I had them. They weren't locked.

I felt such desire for him, such murderous and vengeful desire, that I was trembling. It was difficult to open the handcuffs.

"You think that I'm obsessed with you?" I asked.

"Yes." Not playing now.

"No."

I hooked the handcuff around his wrist, right above the gold watch he'd taken from a dead person, and fastened the other handcuff to the back of the steel garden chair.

"What the fuck are you doing?"

"What do you think?"

He looked down at his wrist.

"Sit in the chair," I said.

I moved in front of him. He had to slide the cuff along the rail of the chair in order to sit down.

I kneeled and opened his belt. Unzipped his fly. He lifted his hip a little, instinctively, helping me. Not something you're supposed to do when you're handcuffed.

I lifted my dress to my waist. I took off my underpants. I stood there, straddling him, my legs on either side of the chair, letting him look at me, close to his face. He did not look away.

His one arm fell to the side of the chair. He closed his eyes as I sank onto him, and he groaned as he arched deep inside of me, engorged now, silent, furious.

He lifted his arm, the arm that was free.

"Don't touch me," I said. My bracelet made a noise against the chair.

"Go on," he whispered. Opening his eyes. "Fuck yourself. I want to watch you fuck yourself."

I moved slowly, his hand now on my ass, his fingers finding me, pushing inside. "Don't," I said. He took away his hand. He moved his pelvis, pushing deeper inside of me, against the clitoris, under the bone. Rocking.

I tried to wait for him. Tried to slow it down, unable to slow it down. He wouldn't oblige me. He watched his cock move in and out of me.

"You like watching," I said.

"Yeah," he said. "I like it in the cut."

When I could not wait any longer, he grabbed me by the hair with one hand. "Okay, okay, okay," he said until it was over.

I lifted my head to look at him.

"Now turn around and do it again," he said. "So I can watch your ass this time. So's I can come."

"No."

He looked at me, deciding.

"Then let me out of these," he said with a smile. Calling my bluff.

"Sure," I said. Calling his bluff. "Where's the key?"

"In my jacket pocket."

I looked around the room.

"On my key ring. In the kitchen."

I lifted myself from him and went into the kitchen. I picked up his jacket and stood with it in the doorway, feeling in the pockets for the keys.

"In the side pocket. Hurry up. I feel like a girl."

I found them. There were other small things in the pocket. Coins. A half-roll of Tums. A bone-handled knife. And a little toy. It looked like a baby carriage.

I held it in my palm, staring at it, not recognizing it. The blood in my body moving slowly. I felt as if I were underwater. Swimming against the current. And then my heart stopped.

"What's the matter?" he asked. "I told you, hurry up."

I held my palm out to him.

"Oh," he said. "I've been meaning to give that to you. I keep forgetting."

"Forgetting?" I still did not understand.

"Take these cuffs off me. They hurt. All those n*****s who used to say it hurt and I never believed them."

"Where did you get this?"

"Get what?"

"This charm."

"I found it on West Broadway. I went back to see if I missed something. I forgot to give it back to you."

"It was you?"

"What?"

"It was you?"

"What the fuck is the matter with you?"

"The girl. The girl with the red hair. The tattoo. I saw it." It was difficult to breathe. I was panting. "But I never thought you killed her."

"The tattoo?" His voice had something new in it. Surprise.

He got slowly to his feet, running his hand along the back of the chair. "Give me the key," he said quietly. He pulled on the cuffs, making the chair jump. "Give me the key," he said again. Dealing with a maniac now. He knew how to do that. Moving toward me slowly, one hand outstretched. Dragging the chair.

He stopped, and put his free hand in his pocket, and the oddity of his position, the humorousness of it, the man handcuffed to the chair, caused me to see him in another way, and once I was able to do that, I was able to move.

I ran out the door and down the stairs, dropping his jacket and the keys on the steps, and ran across the street, running between cars, thinking that I would be safe in the park, with the Jamaicans, already calling to me, what you want, pretty missus?

I looked back at my windows. The walls of my rooms were painted red in the style of 1840. My landlord had been pleased at my choice. So historical. The color made the room look as if it had caught fire.

I ran into someone, and fell to the path. It was someone I thought I knew.

Someone I knew.

Detective Rodriguez. He looked out of place in the park. Not a Rasta. Not a dog owner. Not a junkie.

He took hold of my arm and pulled me to my feet. "Slow down," he said, smiling. "You all right? You need to score that bad?"

I was shaking. "I didn't know." I looked behind me.

"Slow down, slow down, take it easy."

A man came over to us, concerned, and Rodriguez said coldly, "It's all right, she's fine," and the man moved away.

Rodriguez walked me swiftly through the park, toward Sullivan Street, the crowd parting for us as if they knew that it was the smart thing to do. I wondered if they thought I was being arrested. It must have looked that way, the man in the dark suit pulling the crying woman through the park.

He took me to a car, not a police car, parked on the south side of the Square. I knew it was his car because there was a deep gouge across the hood where Lonnie, two n's, had tried to carve her name.

"I can't go with you," I said quickly. "He'd know. We can't go to the police." Shaking my hands as if they were wet.

He laughed. "I am the police."

He opened the door and did not let go of me until I got into the car.

"Why didn't you have it fixed?" I asked suddenly. I

pointed at the scratch on the hood. I realized that I was shouting.

" 'Cause I don't want to forget," he said. He shut my door and came around the front of the car. He took off his jacket and threw it onto the back seat. He locked the doors and started the car, looking across at me quickly as he pulled into traffic. "You all right?" he asked. He rolled up his sleeves as he drove, steering first with one hand, then the other.

He drove west, then north onto the West Side Highway.

I couldn't stop shaking. "It's Malloy," I said.

"What are you talking about?"

"It was Malloy."

He was driving swiftly. "Did he hurt you?"

I shook my head.

The air conditioner was turned high. I rolled down the window.

"Don't do that," he said, reaching across to grab my hand. His fingers pressed the bracelet into my wrist.

For a minute, I could smell the old dirty river. His arm, stretched across me, moved against my breast as he turned the window handle.

He left the highway at 155th Street. There was a bottle of Rémy Martin on the floor and it rolled back and forth on the floor mat. He went down the ramp and turned toward the river, past a construction site with empty trash haulers and bulldozers. I could see the lights of New Jersey across the river. The smell of the water was brackish. We passed a tennis court with a sagging net. Damp fields.

"We're almost there," he said.

"Where are we going?"

"Somewhere we can talk. You can tell me what happened."

There were weeds in the center of the road. The branches of trees dragged against the windshield. I saw black rocks by the side of the road, along the river, rimmed with yellow foam, and I knew that it was low tide.

There was a hollow, ringing sound, and suddenly the bridge loomed from the dark bank, the lights of the cars bouncing off the pylons. The bridge was like a spaceship, shimmering.

He stopped the car in front of a small red lighthouse and turned off the lights. "This is where I come to fish," he said. The lighthouse was like an illustration in a children's book. It had a black door with a lock and chain. There was a spotlight on a pole. He took a duffel bag from the back seat. He got out of the car and walked around to my door. The light shone down on us. He reached in to take my arm and I saw that he had something on the inside of his wrist. Something that was a tattoo.

He unlocked the door of the lighthouse and took me inside. He carried the duffel, the kind of bag you can buy in marine-supply stores. Waterproof. Durable.

It was not dark inside, the big lighted bridge roaring above, the sound of the cars like bees now, swarming.

He did not let go of me. He dropped the bag and with one hand locked the door from the inside.

High on the wall was a window shaped like a porthole. There was a bait box on the ground. A pair of women's high heels on top of the box. An aluminum beach chair, the webbing torn. A saw, not electric, a little rusty. A blue and white Styrofoam chest with New York Giants decals down the sides. Blankets folded neatly. I saw these things very precisely, very exactly, as if their very qualities of density and weight and color would make all the difference to me. I just knew this, that it would make a difference. I didn't try to understand it. I kept it simple. Malloy would have been proud.

He took a barber's straight-edged razor from the bag. Shiny handle. That little metal comma at the end. He put down the bag. He held the razor to my neck. Against the skin.

"You have nice hair," he said. The razor under my chin, his arm fitting neatly between my breasts.

"Thank you."

"Don't thank me. Thank your mom and dad."

I did not feel the razor when he cut me, only knew it an instant later with the sudden rush of heat and pain, the sting of it, the warm blood slaking down my arms and over my hands. It didn't hurt that much after I got used to it. It wasn't a bad cut. Not too bad.

He didn't mean to cut me, he said. But he couldn't help it. Now if I could just hold still, just stop shaking, there wouldn't be so much blood on my dress. I didn't mean to shake. I couldn't stop it. He hadn't meant to cut me.

"*Muy linda. Su pelo.*" He put his hand in my hair, wrapping it around his fist. "You speak Spanish. I know that. That kid Cornelius told me. I never had a girlfriend who could talk Spanish who wasn't Spanish."

"Cornelius?"

"Yeah."

"Why?"

"Why what, *mi ángel*?"

"Why Cornelius?"

He smiled. "I'm a detective. I'm the man." He let go of my hair. "People got to talk to me."

"Take the razor away," I said. Whispering. It was very hot in the lighthouse.

"There's food," he said, pointing to the cooler. Not taking the razor away.

"I don't want food."

"I have to leave you here. People saw us in the park. Just a couple a days. To make it all right. You surprised me, man. I wasn't ready for you yet." He leaned forward to look into my face. "Richie'll take care of you," he said.

Augustina used to say that I had everything in the world but luck. She was wrong. This was luck. Not that he would take care of me, but that he was going to leave me there, take his hands from me, take the razor from my neck. I would get away from that place. The porthole window was out of reach, but there was a metal balcony. A catwalk running around the wall, beneath a skylight. The skylight was broken. Through the glass I could see the bridge, streaked with white light. I could hear the bridge humming.

He rubbed his forearm across my breasts.

"You're not wearing a bra," he said. He slid the razor down my neck, across the hyoid, across the glottis, trailing over the cricothyroid intrinsic muscle, the superior laryngeal nerve, over the little hollow at the center of the clavicle, and I thought of Pauline, my Pauline, and I began to gag. He grabbed me by the back of the neck, pressing the razor against my breast, just under the nipple, the nipple resting on the edge of the blade, the razor cutting smoothly, easily, through the taut cloth, through the skin, the delicate blue skein of netted veins in flood, the nipple cut round, then the breast, opening, the dark blood running like the dark river, the Indian river, the sycamore, my body so vivid that I was blinded. My breast. My breastesses.

"That's what they call a souvenir," I heard him say.

I was blind.

"You should sit down."

He lowered me into the beach chair. The aluminum arms felt cool when I put my arms on them. My arms were wet.

"I'll keep it in my pocket," he said. "That way when I can't be with you I can reach in and feel it, and it will be like we're together." He put it in his pocket.

"How did you know?"

"Know what, *mi amor*?"

"That I saw you with that girl."

"Jimmy told me. Only he don't know it."

"Jimmy?" I couldn't think who he meant.

"He kept saying that maybe you saw something that night you didn't even know you seen. He was driving me crazy. *Loco*. You thought it was Malloy, right?"

"The tattoo."

"We were in Viet Nam together. I was there only forty-one days. I got dysentery, man. They sent me to Hawaii."

I wondered if I knew that.

"And then you got into our car that night. I recognized you right off. I thought you recognized me."

"No." I felt sad.

"She was something, Angela. She sucked the top of my head soft."

"His scar?" My skirt was heavy with blood, pooled between my thighs, seeping slowly through the cotton. It tickled when it dripped onto my skin, into my pubic hair, over the labia. I was not wearing underwear. You remember. "He never would tell me."

"That fucking Malloy." He laughed. "He ruptured his appendix when he was a kid."

My hand over my chest, the blood finding its way between my closed fingers, my ribs light in my warm hand, my breast lighter without the rose nipple to give it weight, to give it meaning.

"Does it hurt?" he asked.

It was difficult to move my head. "All right," I said. "It's all right."

"I have to go now. But I'll be back later. You don't look too good. You like fish?"

Once Augustina and I went to a store in Manila where she had seen a dress that she wanted me to have, a scarlet taffeta dress with big Filipino sleeves and swags of lace caught up with roses. An odd dress for a child. We took it home. My mother said it was ugly and made Augustina take it back. I hadn't even liked the dress, but my mother made me like it. My mother had been jealous of Augustina. "Yes," I said aloud, "that's what it was." My skirt heavy with blood.

"That's not what I fucking asked you," he shouted, startling me. "Do you like fish?"

"The hand. Did you leave it there?"

"The hand?" He looked puzzled. "What the fuck are you talking about?" He walked back and forth in the small space between the wall and the pile of blankets. "You heard that joke about the Garden of Eden?"

I could smell my blood.

"God was looking down, right? and he saw Eve go into

the ocean for a swim and he yelled, oh no, how we going to get the stink out of the fish?"

The handle of the razor gleamed. The light from the bridge hurt my eyes.

"It's a good joke, man," he shouted.

"No."

"It's not a good joke?"

I could see him sometimes, and then I couldn't.

"You want to hear it again?"

"No." I took a breath, holding my head to the side, holding my head to my body.

"It's about fish." He sighed. "I'm sorry," he said. He put his hand on my shoulder. He sounded worried. It confused me. "Sit still," he said.

He stopped suddenly, his head cocked, and looked toward the door. Listening.

There was the sound of cars and trucks on the bridge. The black river. A rat above us on the balcony, its feet clicking on the metal grille. My breath, low, bubbling, harsh, like a big animal giving birth.

He stood listening for several minutes. Several hours. It was hard to measure time. He bent over me, the razor in his hand, and made a quick clicking sound with his tongue and slit my dress down the front, between my thighs. The pooled blood, unpooled, rushed down my legs.

"This dress is a mess," he said in disgust. "I don't *like* cutting you, you know."

Cutting me. He doesn't like it. I don't like it, either. I have a new word for the dictionary. Malloy told it to me. A street word. A word used by gamblers for when you be peepin', he said. In the cut. From vagina. A place to hide. To hedge your bet. But someplace safe, someplace free from harm.

He moved the duffel bag, laying it carefully on top of the blankets, lining them up neatly. "You know why the fishing here is so fucking good? One word."

I waited.

"Chum."

I didn't understand.

"I use my souvenirs for chum sometimes."

He went to the door and leaned against it, his hands flat on it, listening, making sure that there was no one outside. He ran to the metal wall ladder and climbed to the balcony, leaning toward the porthole, shading his eyes with his hands. The bridge zoomed over his head.

I lowered myself to my knees and began to crawl.

He looked down and saw me.

He came quickly down the ladder, opening the razor when he reached the bottom step. "You want me to take another souvenir?"

He grabbed me by the hair and threw his legs around me. Riding me. My hair his reins. He reached down to cover my mouth and I bit his hand. I bit him again. Just like a girl.

I was a girl.

I bit through the skin and he screamed.

He pushed me over, onto my back, and sat on top of me, his knees pressing into my ribs.

I asked him not to hurt me. It seems to be what women say. And men. It did not stop him.

My face. My throat. My breasts. Malloy would know when he saw my hands. My arms. He would know. How I fought.

He lifted himself from me. I heard him unlock the door. For a moment, I felt the cool air from the river, smelling of fish. Smelling of Eve. It made me shudder. I was cold.

There is an essay on the language of the dying. The dying sometimes speak of themselves in the third person. I was not speaking that way. I said: I am bleeding. I am going to bleed to death. And I will be lucky if I die before he returns.

Give me my Scallop shell of quiet.

You know, they did not print the whole of the Indian song in the subway. Only a few lines. But I know the poem.

"It's off in the distance. It came into the room. It's here in the circle."

I know the poem.

She knows the poem.